Troppo

Winner of the 2014 City of Fremantle
T.A.G. Hungerford Award
proudly supported by

Fremantle City Library
A service of City of Fremantle and
Town of East Fremantle

The West Australian

FREMANTLE PRESS
fremantlepress.com.au

First published 2016 by
FREMANTLE PRESS

Fremantle Press Inc. trading as Fremantle Press
PO Box 158, North Fremantle, Western Australia, 6159
fremantlepress.com.au

Cover design Nada Backovic
Cover photograph Sarah Lee, hisarahlee.com Stand-up-paddle athlete
Donica Shouse duck-dives a hand-shaped alaia surfboard under a wave.
This alaia was modelled after the ancient surfboards the Hawaiians surfed
on in the pre-20th century.

 A catalogue record for this
book is available from the
National Library of Australia

ISBN 9781925163803 (paperback)
ISBN 9781925163827 (ebook)

Fremantle Press is supported by the Western Australian State Government
through the Department of Cultural Industries, Tourism and Sport.

Publication of this title was assisted by the Commonwealth Government
through Creative Australia, its arts funding and advisory body.

mantle Press respectfully acknowledges the Whadjuk people of the
Noongar nation as the Traditional Owners and Custodians of the land
where we work in Walyalup.

MADELAINE DICKIE

Troppo

 FREMANTLE PRESS

Some of us willingly live on fault lines.
John Kinsella

'Unwell' ... 'Unwell' ... the diary entries say.
No fuss, no talk of fever, just 'unwell'.
Then at the end no hint of even this.
Geoffrey Lehmann, 'New Guinea Episode'

For Tom

1

The first story I hear about my new boss is in a brothel in Bandar Lampung. I don't realise it's a brothel at first. From the outside it looks like a typical Indonesian beauty salon: pink curtains tacked up in a prayer arch over lace, a gritty 'Salon Kecantikan' sign out the front and a becoming ladyboy at the door, with toilet paper moulded into boobs.

'Hello Missus!' the ladyboy sings, thrusting sideways a sequined hip. 'Bisa saya bantu?' Can I help you?

'Bisa!' The ladyboy leads me to a room furnished with hairdressing chairs and cracked mirrors. There's a girl at one of the mirrors smoothing out a yellow dress that falls just below her undies. She wears cream gloves and stunningly high heels. In a beauty salon in Perth you wouldn't think twice about her outfit. But here in East Sumatra, most women have been covered from head to toe.

She smiles, warily. 'Do you do manicures?' The ladyboy and the girl look at each other; the girl holds her hands behind her back.

'Sorry,' the ladyboy wags his finger from side to side, 'no have manicure.'

'Cream bath?'

'No have.'

'Waxing?'

'No have.'

'Facial?'

'No have.'

'How about a haircut?'

'A haircut?' The girl sounds incredulous.

The ladyboy pouts and picks up a pair of scissors. 'Haircut have!'

Last time I had a cut at a hole-in-the-wall salon my hair looked like the dirty blond wool around the arse of a sheep. 'Well, Pen,' said Josh, 'they made a mess of that.' But Josh isn't here and the bus south to Batu Batur doesn't leave until tomorrow morning. I'd rather spend the afternoon in a beauty salon than nursing my hangover over cups of sweet, weak coffee. 'Alright. Haircut.'

The ladyboy taps his lips with the tips of his pale fingers and murmurs, 'I make you beautiful.'

The girl rolls her eyes and arranges herself on one of the frayed seats.

'So where you from, Missus?' asks the ladyboy. 'Already long-time in Indonesia? You already marry? How many children you have?'

A window drops a sud-coloured square of light onto the floor. Outside, two smog-stunned palms shade a courtyard. Doors are arranged around the courtyard in a similar style to a losmen – a motel – only none of the doors are numbered.

The girl stares through the window.

The ladyboy lifts and looses flaps of my hair.

'Well?'

'Australian. No husband, no children.'

'No children, Missus! Hopefully soon, ya?'

A rattle of hot rain hits the window and the ladyboy glances up. Then he goes back to my hair. 'So where you been in Indonesia?'

'Bali, then a night in Jakarta, now here.'

The ladyboy's eyes blaze. 'Bali! There's many-many party in Bali, ya? Party-party every night!'

I planned on avoiding the Kuta vortex this time, or at least planned on just flirting at the edges of it. Instead, fifty Bintangs and a police chase later …

'Yeah, Bali definitely can be wild.'

'So kenapa kamu disini?' Why you in Lampung? For holiday?

'No, for work. I've got a job.'

'A job? You teach English?'

'I'm going to be managing a surf resort. I don't start for a couple of weeks but I thought I'd come down early, check out the town, have a bit of a break.'

'A resort here in Bandar Lampung?'

'No, Batu Batur.'

At the mention of Batu Batur the girl's head jerks around and her nostrils flare.

The ladyboy casts her a sly look. 'Yuliana used to work in a resort in Batu Batur. Yuliana used to work for Mister Shane. But big problem, ya. She run away here.'

I feel uneasy – Shane's the name of the guy I'll be working for. 'What happened?'

The ladyboy lays down his scissors. The girl bursts out in an angry, rattling dialect. He answers: placating, convincing. Then they fall quiet. The girl tilts her head, just slightly. The ladyboy continues, but softly, 'Mister Shane's Australian, same like you. Yuliana work for him. She work for Mister Shane three year.'

Yuliana is perfectly still. Out in the courtyard one of the doors opens. A man stumbles towards the rear door of the salon, holding a towel over his head.

The ladyboy flicks his tongue over his lipstick and drops his voice to a murmur, 'One night Mister Shane get very, very drunk. They have a big fight, yelling, yelling. Mister Shane think Yuliana stole money from his guests. So he take a knife. Mister Shane take one big knife –'

The man kicks open the door, throws the towel at the girl, then sees me. He stops, his mouth drops. Then he shakes himself.

'Hello Missus!' he says. 'Where you from?'

Fifteen minutes later I pay for the haircut over a counter at the front of the shop. It's better than the last one I had in Indo – just a trim of dead ends with no length lost. Through the open door, steam lifts from the road. There's the smell of roasting satay sticks, of motorbike exhaust and slow-moving sewage. I look back to the ladyboy and lay down an extra fifty thousand rupiah.

'So what did Mister Shane do with the knife?'

The ladyboy's smile flattens. He gestures to Yuliana. Yuliana hesitates, looks at the money, then steps forward and peels back a glove.

She's got no fingers.

2

On the bus south to Batu Batur I vomit for eight hours straight into sandwich-sized plastic bags.

Halfway into the trip, I shit myself.

'Oh fuck. Tell the driver to stop.'

'Sebentar, sebentar.' The conductor up the back waves his hand, palm-down, and lights another kretek cigarette.

He obviously hasn't smelt it yet, but by the time we finally stop at a roadside restaurant, his head is out the window and the seats around me are empty. The restaurant toilets reek of old, pissed-on porcelain. Jumping off the bus here with my gear isn't an option – there are no rooms and no village nearby, only the hazy midday stretch of rice fields and pandanus palms.

If Josh were with me, he'd hold back my hair while I threw up. Then again, if Josh were with me, we wouldn't be travelling by local bus. Despite the explosive bout of Bali belly, I'm glad to be alone.

The bus rattles to life. When you hear the bus start up, it's a sign to get back on. Before long, we're climbing through a chain of viridescent mountains. The sky is pale, moist, the colour of smoked lemon peels. We reach a straight stretch of road and the driver accelerates. The bus goes faster. And faster. And faster. The windows chatter. The women clutch baskets and children on their laps. To our left, there's a long drop into a valley and to our right, a crumbling cliff. Up ahead: a blind corner. The bus groans. We're hurtling toward the corner. My throat tightens. I curl my fingers around the seat in front of me. We swing hard and hit a truck.

*

It takes a couple of hours for the blokes to fix the bus. I sit hunched on the side of the road with a bleeding cheek and a heaving gut, throw bags of vomit into the valley and watch them explode on the rocks below. By the time we reach Batu Batur around midnight, I'm too weak to lift my rucksack onto my back. A man on the bus helps me, then points me in the direction of a losmen.

3

It's hot out on the street. A motorbike sails past, lifting a wing of mud. Across the road a young boy pisses on his toes. I start walking, still dazed with sleep and sick. A wartel. I need to find a wartel to phone Josh. I haven't been in touch since a perfunctory call on my first day in Bali – and the day after, I lost my phone. No doubt he's left messages. No doubt he's worried sick.

Some people lift a hand and yell the ubiquitous and genderless greeting, 'Hello Mister!' Most just stare. Up ahead, the empty racks of a market are wound with plastic and rotting fruit. I quicken my pace when I spot a wartel on the other side.

'Can I call Australia?'

The bloke out the front nods, stubs out his kretek with a toe and leads me inside to the phone box. The walls of the box are on worrying wooden diagonals and the bench inside is chequered with kretek burns and spots of old blood.

'Sebentar,' he says, as he connects the line. Then he gives me another curt nod, 'Sudah.'

A receptionist answers – young and bright and happy. 'I'm sorry. He's just stepped out of the office for lunch. Would you like to leave a message?'

'Can you tell him Penny called?'

'Sure. Penny who?

'He knows who I am.'

'Okay … So would you like to leave a number?'

'No. No number.'

I hang up and go and sit on the doorstep of the wartel. The owner lights a kretek for me and passes it down; it leaves a sweet, clove taste on my lips. Opposite the wartel an old woman is crouched under the shade of a bit of plastic. She swings at a bare-bummed child with her cane. Beyond her there's a row of shops packed with curious clutters of detail: curling cigarette ads, faded fertility bottles, teabags of shampoo, grey gallons of Aqua. Outside the shops is a line of becak riders, folded up in their bicycle taxis. Their dust-coloured legs are cricked and ricked, their hands shade their faces from the sun. Behind the market, behind the suspended, midday town, towers a mountain range.

It's eerie, empty, beguiling.

4

Ibu Ayu and Bapak Joni run five clean bungalows that leave last night's windowless jigsaw of a losmen for dead. The bungalows are on stilts, leaning among stands of frangipani and enclosed by walls of concrete and broken glass. From each balcony there's a view of the heaving reef-ripped ocean.

'There's only one other guest. He's a surfer. French.' Ibu screws up her nose. 'But no problem, you need motorbike? Board hire? Beer? No problem for this, Missus Penny, we happy you to be our guest!'

Ibu Ayu wears a navy jilbab – a headscarf – and the bell curve of a baby swells under her shirt. When she turns to speak to her husband her voice lifts in light, fluty tones, and she touches his hand. It's rare to see gestures of affection between Indonesian couples in public. Bapak Joni takes her fingers and smiles. He has a mouthful of butter-coloured teeth and his t-shirt strains over a rice-big stomach.

By the time I'm finally settling in to my bungalow it's late afternoon. Squalls of salt and spray lift from the ocean and sweep through the palms and window shutters. Despite still feeling sick, I'm happy to be high up, to feel the afternoon moving, gusting around me. And I like the bungalow: its crooked balcony, the white mosquito net that spills over the bed, the geckos in the thatch.

In the top of my rucksack is a pile of clothes still beer-sour from Bali. I'll wash them tomorrow with a bar of soap and a nailbrush. I pull out my medicine bag. Josh would be aghast if he knew it stocked only a single, poisonous bottle. Betadine Cina is legendary among hardcore Indo travellers and surfers, a dark brown liquid that smells like rust and stings like fuck and heals reef cuts, motorbike burns and even sea-ulcers in a matter of days. Next I pull out my high heels, my hair straightener and finally, a few volumes of poetry.

Once everything is in its place, I feel better. To inhabit a temporary space like this, you have to make an imprint, have to neutralise the energy of all the other travellers who've slept there before you. Although it's only been an hour, there's more of me here than in a year of living with Josh. The interior of his apartment in Scarborough was nearly bare, the furniture spare, the paint job neutral. But it smelled good, like finely ground coffee, citrus, Calvin Klein.

I crash on the bed. The fan turns slack yellow circles in the air. Josh is probably at home cooking dinner. He's an epic cook, turning out contemporary gourmet dishes that put my slapdash stir-fries to shame. If I were home we'd be eating together, then doing the dishes and settling in to watch the ABC's *Foreign Correspondent*. Josh loves the quiet rituals of domesticity. Sometimes it's too much. I end up out midweek, loose and wild at a work party or with the girls at a bar, throwing my eyes and talking to strangers, unable to bear the thought of another unvaried evening. He says it's fine, says I should go out with the girls and do some more solo travel, says he understands how important it is to do this at my age. He's fourteen years older than me. Says he'll wait.

5

On Ibu's recommendation I head to town for a feed at the night market. I'm feeling a little better and reckon I can stomach something light. It's early evening and the market is being set up. Light bulbs flicker above warming vats of oil, and kaki lima are wheeled into place. From the outside, kaki lima look like wooden trolleys, but when unfolded, all sorts of compartments jump open, revealing gas bottles, pipes, drawers full of chilli, noodles, rice. Portable restaurants. 'Portable genius,' Josh said after his first thirty-cent meal at a kaki lima in Denpasar. He admired the Indos' inventiveness, though scowled over the unhygienic food prep. 'That woman just used her fingers. Jesus, Penny, do you really think you should eat that?' This sort of caution gave me the shits. As did his refusal to eat anywhere other than the tourist restaurants in the last two weeks of our trip.

After I've done a lap of the market, I perch on a wooden stool in front of a kaki lima selling bakso.

'Lima minut lagi,' the man says. Five more minutes.

The night air is sticky as cut mango.

A local bloke with a sparse but ambitious moustache comes and sits next to me.

'Hello Mister! Where you from?' he asks, resting the side of his foot on his knee and lighting a kretek.

'Australia.'

'You can speak Indonesian?'

'I can.' As a fifteen year old I lived with Dad in Bali for almost a year. Talk about going off the rails. But one good thing to come of it was a near-fluent grasp of the language.

The bakso seller looks up from his pot. 'Sudah pintar,' he affirms.

So we chat and I become animated, eager to move my tongue around the language again. When the man asks if I'm married and how many children I have, I invent three husbands and eight children. The bloke looks utterly bewildered. He shakes my hand without meeting my eyes, says, 'Good to meet you Mister,' and walks off.

That's when I notice him. He's leaning against the kaki lima stand, lifting my bowl of bakso, passing it down to me. 'Eight kids, eh?'

I grin and raise a spoonful to my lips.

'You mind if I join ya?' He pulls up a stool. 'I'm Matt.'

My lips are tingling with chilli. 'Penelope.'

'Nice to meet ya, Penny.'

By this time it's dark. The air is smoky with frying fish scales. Matt's cheek and jaw are kerosene-lit. Not quite handsome.

'You live here?' I ask, after a slow mouthful.

'Yeah, on and off. At the moment on.'

He's in his late twenties or early thirties. Older than me, younger than Josh. He speaks with a slow, sun-damaged drawl – one Aussie expats often affect in the tropics.

'What about yourself? You here for long?'

Work kicks off in a few weeks and then six months, a year? I told Josh I didn't know how long I'd be away.

Well what does that mean? he'd demanded. What does that mean for us?

I dunno, I said. I dunno. You tell me.

Matt's looking at me expectantly.

'Ahh … maybe like, maybe for a while.'

'Oh yeah.' He nods, like it's a perfectly coherent answer. 'So where are you staying?'

'Just at those bungalows on the beach.'

'Ibu Ayu's, eh? She's lovely. But steer clear of Shane's Sumatran Oasis if you can. It's the other main tourist accom here, bit out of town.'

There's a tapping in my blood. I wasn't convinced by the ladyboy's story in Bandar Lampung about the girl's fingers; I know how ladyboys can be inclined to melodrama. 'Oh yeah? Why's that?'

A couple of men crouch nearby in red, grease-stained singlets. Their hands hang between their knees, their heads are cocked.

'To put it bluntly, the bloke who runs it is a real crazy fucker. Because of him, Batu Batur's in a pretty tense state. The expatriates are barely tolerated as is, let alone blow-ins like yourself.'

The insult stings. 'I'm *not* a blow-in! I've got a job here!' But his attention has been caught by a bloke riding up to us on the coughing skeleton of a motorbike.

'Permisi, Mister Matthew!'

The black heat from the exhaust scorches my shins. They're hairy. They need a shave. Hopefully it's too dark to notice.

'Mister Matthew! Ayo pulang.'

'Now?'

'Sekarang, yuk!'

Matt stands up. 'Righto, Penny. I'll catchya later.'

He drops me a wink and swings his leg over the bike.

'Seeya.' I give him a casual smile and go back to my bakso.

But I'm still thinking about him later that night, as the rain slips cool down the thatch.

6

Ibu Ayu sets my breakfast on the dining deck. It seems the Frenchman prefers to eat alone. Or maybe he's already gone for a wave. I wrap my fingers around a glass of basalt-coloured coffee and we gossip. Our talk whirls from women's business to the business of the bungalows, from the surly Frenchman to traditional Lampung weavings. I want to find some weavings for Dad – he collects Indonesian kain ikat and kain songket. Ibu Ayu says she knows some women who might show me their work and that she'll ask them at the morning market.

'Did you grow up in Batu Batur?' I ask.

'Ya, of course!' she tells me proudly. 'I spend three year at university in Bandar Lampung, studying tourism and English. Then I meet Joni and we come back here to start business.'

'Were there already tourists visiting Batu Batur back then?'

Ibu furrows her brow. Her skin is flawless: it probably won't wrinkle until she's well into her sixties.

'Ya, not so many.'

A quiet grows between us. The garden is jammed with wild, edible, wet colours. Nothing here is for decoration, everything has utility, from the row of pandanus palms along the back wall to the mango and papaya trees. We sit comfortably. My Indonesian friends aren't scared of silence. As the seconds unfold, I think again of my future boss and wonder what Ibu Ayu thinks about him. The best way to approach difficult topics here is always slowly, and so I work toward the question by asking how many other surf resorts there are in the area, and if the owners are locals or bules like myself and then finally, if she's heard of anyone called Shane.

When Ibu Ayu hears the name Shane she reacts explosively, nearly knocking over my coffee glass with her closed fist. 'Mister Shane, he no good! He already long-time live here. But Ibu think not much longer.'

'What, why? What's he done?'

'He say to local people: no more fishing off beach because beach is for tourist! He say to them: no more using channel for boats, because channel for surfers! No good. Local people, they no like Mister Shane. And they no like the tourist so much either.' She slaps off a mosquito, leaving a smudge of blood. Then, realising what she's said, she adds quickly, 'But you can speak Indonesian and you staying here with me, so I thinking you safe, no problem.'

'Does he have a wife?

Ibu looks at me almost pityingly. 'What woman would put up with Mister Shane? He did have wife, Chinese wife, but she try kill herself. So he send her back to China. Now, sometimes he pay Javanese girl, girl from Medan, or Lampung, okay. They stay little while, then they take the money, and go, go, faraway, quick!'

A few chooks wander the garden. They inspect, peck, and flick at the earth, gurgling in their throats.

Ibu lowers her voice. 'Maybe five month ago, people say he cut the fingers off a girl for stealing.'

'What girl? Was she okay?'

Ibu adjusts her headscarf. 'This girl, no-one know her. She from somewhere else, some other village, maybe from Java. She orang lain, kan?'

Orang lain. Not from here. An outsider. A blow-in.

'It happen, then she run away. No-one see her since.'

I'm desperate for the story not to be true but it seems unlikely, given the matching story of the girl in the brothel. 'That's awful, Bu. Has Shane been here long?'

'Nearly ten year. He have surf camp here. Before that, he live in Aceh. Ten year too long, Penny. He no good for this town, no good for the tourist. He crazy man, orang gila! But how come you hear of Mister Shane? You want to go surfing there? Maybe stay at his surf resort?'

Should I tell Ibu Ayu? I might learn more by staying quiet. But she'll find out anyway so it's probably better she hears it from me. I'd hate for her to think me dishonest, think I'm the same as him or any other dodgy expats who may have washed up here. There's certainly no shortage of foreign con artists, speculators and drunks in Bali, and Batu Batur probably isn't that different. So I tell her outright, 'Actually, I've got a job working at Shane's.'

Her eyes widen for a moment.

'Yeah, I start soon as his new manager.'

Ibu stands, picks up our glasses. 'Oh 'gitu,' she says. It's like that, is it? 'Maybe you should talk to Joni ya, Joni tell you what Shane did when he first come to Batu Batur.'

After that she becomes cautious around me, warm, but not overly intimate. We don't speak of Shane again.

7

It's those crushing hours in the middle of the day, those dead hours when it's too hot to move. I lie under a wet sarong with a pain like yanked-out urchin spines behind my eyes. Sweat through everything: pillows, sheets, bra, singlet. The fan barely cutting the torrid air. And the loneliness. In the back of my throat. Wondering, wandering thoughts about Josh, about ex-lovers, remembered conversations, mad friends. And knowing while they're in my thoughts I'm not in theirs. So what the hell am I doing here, alone? Why do I always bolt when things get too hard, relationships too serious? Why am I never happy with what I've got, where I am, always jerked along by whim and the conviction there's something better just ahead? And then, most pressingly, what am I going to do if these stories about Shane are true?

The dead hours.

8

I roll from under the mozzie net, slam half a litre of water and head out for a walk. The Frenchman's in the garden. He has his surfboard across his knees and is applying a fresh coat of wax with long rhythmic strokes. He gives me the faintest nod. Although we're the only guests, he refuses to be lured into conversation – he is somber-eyed, a remorseful Bertrand Cantat.

A blue door at the end of the garden leads onto the beach. The bungalows are in line with a ramshackle row of fishermen's shacks and palms. On the other side of the reef, waves are crosshatched to the horizon. Clouds hang hot and low. To the south, a cholera-coloured river rips a wide channel through the sand. I walk north, toward the point where the coast curves and volcanoes shear into sea.

There are all sorts of things coughed up on the sand. A pair of thongs. The red foil of a Beng-Beng wrapper. A sodden nappy. Then there are the organs: the hearts and kidneys and livers of old coral. The sand is coarse, slippery. With each step, I sink to my ankles.

Up ahead, two women balancing baskets on their heads move toward me with an easy, swinging grace.

'Hello Mister!' The woman's skin is black from sun and she squints, one hand on her basket, one on her hip.

'Mau ke mana Mister?' asks her friend. Where are you going?

Like many of the women here, she has high, sculpted cheekbones – almost Nepalese.

'Jalan-jalan,' I reply. Just walking. 'Mau ke mana?'

They gesture toward Batu Batur. Then the younger woman with the enviable cheekbones asks, 'Sendirian?' Are you alone?

I smile and shrug and say yeah, but no worries.

The women look at each other and shake their heads.

'Hati-hati, ya,' they murmur. Be careful.

'Kenapa?' Why?

'Ada orang gila.' They cast fearful looks to the line of jungle and fishing shacks, then adjust their baskets, give me uneasy smiles and continue on their way.

Their warning hangs behind them, vaguely unpleasant, like the tang in the air after insect spray. Surely I don't need to be worried about some madman. Travelling in remote places I've often been asked where my husband is; I'm often warned to be careful.

After a while, I see some fishermen up near the palms repairing a net. They regard me with narrowed eyes.

'Mau ke mana?' calls one of the men.

'Jalan-jalan,' I reply.

'Sendirian?

'Yeah I'm alone.'

The men click and look further up the beach. 'It's getting dark,' one says.

I laugh off his concern and keep walking, but a cactus of unease flowers in my gut. Waves break over the reef with back-snapping force and there's no-one surfing. There's no-one.

Then suddenly I catch a dark flicker of movement among the palms. I stop. Look directly at the dusky undergrowth. Nothing. No, there's nothing moving. Perhaps it was a bird. A monkey. I start walking again, but more slowly this time.

When I lived in Kuta with Dad, I had a room on the second storey of our house. Often on dawn or dusk, I noticed, at the corner of my eye, crouching silhouettes, penumbras without form. 'Hantu,' my Balinese friends whispered. Spirits.

When I challenged the shadows face-on, or blinked, they disappeared, leaving a faint chill, the smell of petrol, a pile of crumbled incense sticks.

I shiver. I'm a long way from Ibu Ayu's, and the last fishermen's huts are at least half an hour behind me. The water bracketed inside the reef is like a sheet of olive glass and, above it, the clouds are beginning to gnar with dusk and rain.

That's when I see the shape again. This time it doesn't disappear. It's a man. Standing there. Watching me. He drops to a crouch. He eases off his pants. His pale fingers wrap delicately around his cock.

I tuck my skirt into my undies, scrunch the strap of my bag into my fist, and run.

9

Finally, soaked with sweat and rain, I fall through the blue door to Ibu Ayu's garden, then slip and trip on one of the steps. My palms skid out and I land chin-first in the mud. There are footsteps. I lift my chin, hoping with all my heart it isn't the Frenchman.

It is.

'Mademoiselle?' He touches my elbow in enquiry, a laugh rippling under his features. 'Would you like a towel, a drink?'

'Can't think of anything I'd like more.'

He puzzles his brow, so I tell him, 'Oui!' and follow him up to his balcony. He goes inside his room and comes back a moment later with a towel and a t-shirt.

'Un moment.' Then he goes back into his room and reappears with a bottle of gin, a can of tonic, a plate of lime and two short glasses.

'Is warm.'

'No worries.'

I towel off the mud as best I can, settle into one of the plastic chairs.

Fear and shame melt into relief.

'I'm Emile,' he says, reaching out his hand.

'Penelope.'

Emile snaps the can. There's the quick fizz of tonic on gin. We sip, slowly, to the purling sound of rain.

10

After breakfast the next day, I go back to the wartel. The owner lifts an eyebrow and gestures me into the box. Then he sits outside to listen. I dial Josh's work number.

'Josh.'

'Penny! Where are you? I've been worried sick. Don't you have internet? What happened to your phone? I've left god knows how many messages. You said you'd call as soon as you got to Batu Batur! I keep asking Mandy, has Penny called?'

'But I did call!' I say hotly. 'Your new receptionist *obviously* didn't pass on my message!'

The wartel bloke fires up a kretek, eyes sliding sideways in interest. Josh doesn't say anything and an awful pause grows. The bright red numbers bump upward, indicating the rising cost of the call: Rp100, Rp1000, Rp10,000.

'Well, alright then, I'll have a word to her,' Josh finally says. 'So. Are you okay?'

I think about yesterday at the beach, about drinking in silence with the Frenchman until midnight. I think of the bus accident and of being sick and of meeting Matt.

'Yeah.' The numbers have hit Rp30,000. Four dollars. Red font, sans serifs. 'You?'

He started it wrong and now there's ugliness, awkwardness between us, the kind that can only be resolved through sex. Not over the phone. Not from Sumatra.

'Yeah, good,' he says.

'I miss you.' It sounds insincere, so I rush on. I ask about the new receptionist, his company, the flat. All good, he says. Work's good, he says. A sick pause, then he asks about Bali, what it was like catching up with my old schoolfriends.

'Mellow,' I lie. 'Super mellow.'

I tell him I've been crook, that the new boss sounds like an arsehole and the town doesn't really feel safe. Josh encourages me to stick it out, says it'll be a great experience, that I should make the most of it.

He's always so measured, so reasonable.

'Jesus,' I sigh into the phone, half-joking, 'you sound like my dad.'

He goes silent.

'I mean, Josh … I didn't mean …'

Rp115,000.

The wartel owner flicks the butt of his cigarette out the door. Red cinders fade on concrete.

At last Josh says, 'Call me again in a couple of days, okay?'

The receipt inches through the machine.

Twenty bucks.

Outside, the same old woman whacks the same small child with a cane. I decide to call back but the man tells me the electricity has dropped out.

'Banyak duit,' he says slyly, 'calling Australia. Australian people have many-many money, ya? Not like Indonesians.' He strokes his moustache. 'How much you pay, ticket from Australia to Lampung?'

11

Back at the bungalows there's a girl pushing a broom. She glances up, returns my wave with a shy smile. Then I bounce up the stairs to my balcony two at a time, kick off my thongs and collapse into a chair. Over the fence the ocean is the colour of old soap. Against the line of palms are the shapes of several blokes. Uneasiness sets in. I close the book on my lap. They look like wooden wayang golek puppets: crouching, stretching, flexing. They look like they're watching me.

I shut my eyes. The conversation with Josh is still making swing-dizzy circles in my head. If only I'd been more supplicating, humoured him, hadn't said that fucking thing about him sounding like my dad. My age is the only thing he's self-conscious about. When it was just the two of us it didn't matter so much, but I could sense it when we had dinners or barbies with his friends, sense his unspoken expectation that I complement him, not embarrass him, not say anything stupid. Once, before we got out of the car, he even went so far as to advise me that maybe I should listen more, should think before I speak, should remember that his friends were bank managers, councillors, small business owners; should watch my language and maybe, just *maybe*, should consider staying sober. That particular night I really went for it. While toddlers crashed into the legs of the dining table, their mothers – chairs angled away from me – talked endlessly about renovations and how much they paid for their plasma televisions and which private schools they were enrolling their children at. Most of these women knew Josh's ex-wife, some had even gone to school with her. They judged him for hooking up with me so soon after the separation. I never stood a chance of being accepted.

I sullenly drained a bottle of white and then, working by finger-widths through a bottle of Captain Morgan, my tongue turned nasty. I was obnoxious and fixing to fight.

Josh didn't speak to me for two days.

That was a month ago.

On the first day of the silent treatment, I found the job at Shane's advertised on the internet, and applied. On the second day, before even hearing back from Shane, I booked a ticket to Indo.

Josh took the news in his usual, measured manner, offering his one hundred percent support. But the night before I left I caught him sobbing on the edge of the bathtub, head bent and shoulders slack. I tried to nudge onto his lap, in my hot pink Brazilian undies, but he gently pushed me back through the door.

I open my eyes.

The men are still there, watching me.

And Matt's turned up.

It takes a moment for me to recognise him – the kerosene-lit memory of his face is a fraction of what he looks like in the flat midday light. He calls out to Bapak Joni. Bapak emerges from behind one of the buildings, an axe in his hand. After greeting, the men's faces become drawn and intense. Whatever they're talking about is serious. Matt senses he's being watched; he breaks off the conversation and glances around. I drop my eyes, face burning. A few minutes later there's the creak of balcony steps. Matt's head appears, a mane of sand-coloured curls.

'How's it goin', Pen?'

'Alright.' I put my book on the table. It's a new book of poetry by Zan Ross called *en passant*. Each poem is like a single stick of dynamite, sea and sex.

Matt doesn't glance at the book. He falls into the chair next to me and stretches out his legs. They're long, tanned, braided with scars.

We sit for a while in an easy silence. Over the garden the air is thick with dragonflies. They float, juicy and fat and red. The afternoon is still, tepid, and now sharp with his smell.

'It's amazing, isn't it,' he says after a while, 'the way the Indos open you. You can be sitting down for a feed and someone will come up and sit next to you and ask how are you? where are you going? what's your name? You're constantly being opened, constantly have to share. It's not like back in Aus where people don't give a shit.'

'Yeah, fully. So whereabouts are you from?'

'I guess I've probably spent the most time in WA – down around Margs.'

His accent has the flat rustle of leaves, fires, flies. It's the kind of accent you'd swoon over if you'd been overseas for a while.

'But,' he continues, 'I didn't grow up in Australia. When I was a kid my parents worked in the Solomon Islands and Vanuatu.'

'No way.'

His eyes are trained on the ocean. Waves roll in over the reef, white with midday and shiny as cans. 'What about yourself?'

'I'm living in Perth at the moment but grew up in Albany. And I had a year in Bali when I was fifteen. How come you're in Batu Batur?'

'The surf, mainly. Over the years I've been surfing Bali, G-Land, the Mentawais. But those places are fucked now, too many tourists. And the locals have got a taste for cash. I wanted to get away from that shit. Somewhere a bit more remote.' He crosses his ankles. 'I first came here five years ago. Was scoping out some other spots to live in the Philippines and Java, but I reckon this is it. If the government can keep a lid on those terrorist groups, this place could be the next G-Land. But at the moment I don't reckon it's that safe.'

I take a stab. 'Is that because of Shane?'

'In Batu Batur, I reckon it's directly 'cause of Shane.' He gives me a hard, disarmingly intimate look. His eyes are grey. Or maybe green. A subtle underwater colour.

There's so much I want to ask him. Like, what's the deal with Shane? What was it like growing up in the South Pacific? What did his parents do? How long has he been here, how long is he staying, are there terrorist groups here?

But these questions will have to wait because for the moment we're skimming, skimming in the way you have to before you can circle back, start talking with depth.

'Are you working here as well?'

'Yeah, I'm a pilot.'

'A pilot!'

More questions!

'With Siliwangi Air. They fly out of Bandar Lampung.'

'Yeah, right. So you're obviously not working at the moment?'

'Nah, got a few weeks off. Have a place here in the village.' He makes a vague gesture in the direction of town.

'Cool. So where's the most interesting place in Indo you've flown?'

His tongue rests on his top teeth for a moment. They're straight, white, strong. 'That's a hard one, Pen. But I'd have to say Nias and probably Timor Leste.'

'Why?'

'Well, the last time I flew to Nias with a local crew, some

hectic stuff was going down. Old, old rituals, black magic, human sacrifices, shit like that.'

He waits for my derision, for another question, but now I'm silent. The stories that come out of Nias are not the kind of stories you laugh at. Not the kind of stories you forget.

'So anyway, the Javanese crew I flew with refused to go back on a second run. Said it was too dangerous. The flight path ended up being scrapped. I personally didn't see anything. But the place has a weird feel about it.'

'And how about Timor?'

'Christ,' he says. 'What can I say about Timor? For years the Australian government did *nothing* about Indo's occupation, too busy licking Soeharto's balls to keep "stability in the region". And then in ninety-nine... Did you know that the hills around Dili are bald? No trees grow on them. When the Timorese fled the capital to hide in the hills – we're talking children, women, elderly people – the Indos dumped chemicals on them. Fucken chemicals. Anyway. What are you up to tomorrow night?'

I shrug, trying to appear nonchalant.

'I've been invited to a barbie. Just with some local crew and some bules who own land and have houses here. I was wondering if you wanted to come with me?'

'Sure!'

Perhaps it comes out too eager. I'm aware of the way he fills the space next to me. He smells like man and salt; present but not present, vamped by the close proximity of the sea. Something stirs in my gut. I'd like to whip him into long dangerous conversation, like to open him, the same way the Indos open us, only much more deeply.

But he's standing up, stretching his legs, lifting my Aqua bottle to his mouth.

'See ya tomorrow then,' he says, wiping his mouth with the back of his hand. He catches my eyes and holds them.

'What time do you reckon you'll swing past?' I say.

Grey intimacy quickly turns to tease. 'Jam karet, sayang!'

I laugh, embarrassed. Of course. 'Rubber time'. Matt might turn up at five tomorrow night, or at six, or at seven.

'Oi, Pen,' he says as he's halfway down the steps.

'Yeah?'

'You surf?'

'Not since I moved to Perth. Hoping to get back into it, though.'

He reaches the grass, looks back up. 'We should go for a wave together.'

'Awesome, I'd love to!'

'Cool. You're on.'

He turns and walks through the garden to the front gate, nodding to Ibu Ayu as he passes. She continues to fan herself with a bit of old newspaper. Then she turns her face to me and shakes her head.

12

Ibu and I walk to the morning market together. One hand steadies the empty basket on her head, the other steadies her belly.

'Masih lama?'

'Not long,' she replies, 'maybe six week. Hopefully we lucky, hopefully this one a boy. Penny punya berapa saudara?'

'Just one sister. Younger.'

'But no boys?'

'No.'

She laughs in disbelief.

I haven't been up this early for a couple of months. Leading up to Indo, I was working at a backpackers in the city for at least a night a week and did the close shift at a pub in Cottesloe on the weekends. Although I usually got home around two, I didn't have any trouble sleeping through Josh's mobile phone alarm. He set it for five thirty every morning so he could train.

Now, despite the fact it's still dark, it seems as if no-one's in bed. Women sweep piles of rubbish into the gutters then set them alight, and all along the street is the soft, black crackle of plastic. As we near the market there's a sudden detonation of white noise, feedback from the mosque's PA. The muezzin's voice lifts rich and sonorous. When he pauses for breath, the call to prayer from dozens of other mosques can be heard drifting ash-like down the mountain valleys.

'Mau pisang goreng?' Ibu asks as we reach the first kaki lima at the edge of the market. A blinking yellow bulb is suspended above a pan of spitting oil. Battered bits of banana are slowly turning gold.

'Definitely!'

Ibu orders two thousand worth and the vendor hands us a warm paper bag transparent with oil.

The morning markets are busy. Women turn fruit over in their hands, men sip coffee from plastic cups and children scamper figure eights in their pyjamas. In the parking lot, buses are loaded with screaming goats and baskets of petrol-coloured fish. It's just after five and the market is in full swing. It makes sense to start early; this is the only time of day it's cool enough to do anything.

Ibu moves off to barter for some vegetables and I crouch in front of an old woman selling rambutans. They're stacked neatly on a batik sarong; cool, spiny sunsets, red and gold and chartreuse.

'Ya, ya, enak!' The old woman is buzzing on betel nut; she nods enthusiastically and licks a set of vintage-red teeth. None of the younger women in Batu Batur chew betel. They don't seem to like the idea of accessorising their jeans or jackets with red mouthfuls of teeth.

'Berapa?' I ask.

The woman quotes an honest price so I don't bother haggling. I scoop them into my bag and look around for Ibu. She's gossiping with a friend.

Her friend touches the tips of her fingers to the tips of my fingers and smiles. Then Ibu excuses us and we move off, bumping past stands of cassettes and combs. She tells me there's only one woman selling kain ikat at the market that morning but in a couple of days there'll be more. We have a look at it anyway:

the woman has four pieces but the fabric is in poor condition, stippled with mould.

After lapping the market, Ibu and I walk home. The morning sun is watery; it flickers through the fronds of the coconut trees as if reflecting off a puddle. Over the last few days the rain has held off until two or three in the afternoon. Then it has dropped in sheets, whitely, blindingly, until five or six in the evening.

'Would you like to see something?' Ibu asks when we get back to the bungalows.

'Of course!'

'Wait here.'

The girl I saw yesterday is in the kitchen. She looks up at me, curious. She's about sixteen.

'Who's that?' I ask when Ibu returns, carrying a bundle in her arms.

'My sister's daughter. Cahyati. She's here to work. My sister live in the mountains but have five other children, so not much money for the food. So that one coming here, one, maybe two years.' She shrugs and places the bundle carefully on the tabletop. Inside is an extraordinary old tapis weaving. Shimmers of gold thread are worked through earthy bands of colour. Distilled in this textile is the whole process of its becoming: silk cocoon for silk yarn, wax from a beehive for stretching the yarn, the root of lemongrass as a preserving agent. The colours are drawn painstakingly from the bark of trees. Rambutan for the black, durian for the chocolate, betel nut for the reds. At the bottom of the tapis is an unusual fringe of mirrors and cowrie shells.

Dad would love this piece.

Ibu is looking at my face intently, waiting for a response.

'Kasih ke saya!' I joke. 'As an oleh-oleh.' Give it to me, as a souvenir!

How many times have I been asked to hand over skirts and

sunnies and shirts and purses?

Satisfied, Ibu tells me she wore it at her wedding. Before her, her mother had also worn it, as had her grandmother and her great-grandmother. 'If this one is a girl,' she pats her stomach, 'she will wear it next.'

Given its age, it's in good condition. Most old Indonesian weavings are preserved in museums. The climate here, the hot wet air, chews into fabrics and rots them – like the weavings I'd been shown at the morning market. It's difficult to find pieces over fifty years old. But this weaving has been well looked after. I feel humbled by how long it's been in Ibu Ayu's family, by that ritualistic connection she has to her ancestors.

Dad holds a reverence for material artefacts or heirlooms, but to us he passed on the immaterial – wild tales told to my sister Lucy and I on camping trips along the Fitzgerald Coast. When he got started, Mum would sigh. We'd hear about how he weathered a cyclone on a leaky copra boat in PNG; how in Madagascar there were spiders the size of dinner plates that chased your shadow. We'd hear stories about Indonesia: puppet shows that went all night in the palace in Yogyakarta, how he'd stomached a thick mix of pig's blood and chilli at a wedding in Ubud, how you used to be able to buy bags of hash from topless Frenchwomen in Kuta. 'Enough!' Mum would say at this point. 'Girls, shut your ears.' If he was feeling slack on the storytelling front, we got poetry. Dad especially dug Snyder and Baxter, enthralled us with poems about sea lions, swamps and fog; the flavour of sandstone, and cold like strychnine in the veins.

'Mau kopi?' Ibu asks, carefully folding the tapis.

'I'd love a coffee.'

'Cahyati!' Ibu yells toward the kitchen.

Cahyati appears, wiping her hands on a tea towel.

'Kopi hitam,' Ibu jerks her head at me.

Cahyati turns without a sound.

The coffee arrives at the same time as some other travellers, a dirty dreadlocked trio, one Pommie and two chisel-faced German girls. They demand Ibu Ayu move another bed into the bungalow so the three of them can sleep in one room to cut the cost. Ibu Ayu relents but tells them they can move the bed themselves. I drain my coffee, slide from my seat and go and find Bapak Joni.

Joni is in the car park crouched next to a motorbike, a silver fan of tools at his toes.

'Hey Joni! What are you up to?'

He gestures to the bike and tells me a bule fell into a river on it a couple of weeks ago.

'Fell into a river!' I exclaim. 'What an idiot! How did that happen?'

His fingers move deftly around the spark plugs, chopping, changing, rearranging. 'Who knows,' he says with a wry smile.

I crouch nearby in the shade, watch for a bit, wonder how to begin.

Joni begins for me, slipping in to Indonesian. 'So my wife tells me you've got a job with Shane?'

Relieved, I rush, 'Yeah, yeah, I start next week. Ibu said you had a bit to do with Shane when he first moved here?'

Joni doesn't meet my eyes and speaks slowly, but as his story gathers momentum so does his pace. Joni was the first local to surf here. Well, not quite local, both his parents were Javanese but he grew up in Batu Batur. When he was a kid, some Aussie surfers had come through the area and he offered to be their guide. He says he was amazed, watching them surf, says he'd never seen people having so much fun. Every time the boys came in from the water for rice and fish, he asked to have a go of a board. Eventually, when they headed off to the Mentawais, they left one for him. Despite it being bruised from water damage, badly patched up after dings with coral, it was still a board, and Joni taught himself to surf. When Shane turned up maybe five years later, there was only a trickle of surfers passing through and Joni was stoked to have someone to paddle out with. He took Shane to every unnamed, pitching wave he'd discovered. Shane repaid him by bullying and bribing his way onto a piece of land that had originally been a national park. The land fronted a perfect right-hand wave with a fast, whackable wall and the occasional barrel section. Once the deal was sealed and construction was underway, Shane banned Joni from paddling out at 'his' spot. Told him if he wanted to surf there, he'd have to pay, or be staying at his resort.

'So what did you do? Weren't you furious at him?'

'Ya, in every country there are good and bad people. Not all bule are like Mister Shane.'

'But what about people in this town, why don't they just get rid of him?'

Joni's face flushes. 'Bribes,' he says. 'Shane gives the police bribes.'

'But most business owners pay bribes to the police, don't they, for "security", to stay open, if they're serving alcohol?'

'Yeah, but Shane pays them even more.'

I think about this for a moment, then ask, 'Joni, do the local people like having bules here?'

Joni wipes his hands on a rag. 'Here, they're still village people. Their thinking is primitive.'

I'm shocked for a moment at his choice of words, before remembering that his family is Javanese. The Javanese are notorious for their snobbery, their belief that they are culturally superior, more sophisticated than people in other parts of the archipelago.

He says, 'Maybe they see the tourists here, see them surfing, doing nothing, while they work hard seven days a week. And then they see a bule like Shane … For me, I always think one day my children might go to Australia and I hope people there are kind to them. So I try and help the foreigners here to find the waves, see the waterfalls, the culture. We have to be friendly, to be open, to give. That's what our religion teaches us.'

What kind of reception would his children receive if they ever made it to Australia? If they walked into the local at Armadale or Bunbury I wonder if they'd be told to go home, to stop stealing our jobs?

It's funny, you always think of the other as being in relation to yourself. You never imagine that *you* could be that other.

13

Matt comes after the rain. It's taken me an hour to get ready. I've fixed my hair with the straightener so it hangs blond and neat down my back and found a lipstick that matches my dress. The dress is strapless and dark red, totally fine for Bali, but hopefully not too dressy for this party, too indiscreet for the motorbike ride.

Matt whistles when he sees me, then bends down and kisses my cheek.

'Fuck, you look smokin' hot!'

I tingle with pleasure.

'So, ah, where's Penny then?'

I laugh and appraise him quickly, not bold enough to give him the same lecherous once-over.

'I like your shirt.' It's patterned with an unusual green and white latticework.

'Yeah?' He twists his arm and inspects the sleeve, pleased. 'I got it made when I was in China. Just picked the fabric and gave it to a tailor.'

'Oh yeah! When were you in China?'

We wander through the garden and out the front gate, chatting. About the Chinese, Indos and travel. I jump on the motorbike behind him. His hair is pulled into a sun-bleached ponytail. It smells washed.

'Hold on,' he says.

I rest my fingers lightly on his stomach.

'Nah,' he says, 'hold on!'

We head for the mountains. As we climb, I lift my face to the sky. There's something blissful about letting someone else be in control, especially when they're a good rider. I've had some horrific experiences as a passenger in Bali. I slid under a car on Jalan Legian with my mad Japanese schoolmate Haruki. The side of my knee and shoulder were left sticking to the asphalt. But nothing close to this ever happened with Josh. He refused to even get on a motorbike, insisted on hiring a car and driver whenever we went anywhere.

I rest my cheek on Matt's back.

The air becomes cooler. Vines and trees with flat, dark leaves make a tunnel over the road. Every now and then the vegetation breaks, revealing blue, twilit valleys, kilometres wide. My imagination goes wild; the last Sumatran tigers are in there, moving silky and dangerous through the undergrowth. There are remote villages hidden among the trees; dukuns murmuring magic in lightless shacks; the fabled and feared hairy people, goat people.

Matt says something over his shoulder.

'What!?'

'There's a waterfall near here. And some hot springs. We should check 'em after the party.'

We pass a cluster of daft dancing children: they flick purple tongues and blind eyes after us. Then, as we near a pile of durians on the side of the road, Matt swings off onto a dirt track. The track leads to a house ringed with wooden balconies and lit with kerosene lamps. He cuts the engine and we both sit for a moment, staring at the lights. The walls of the house are made of glass and from here all we can see are the silhouettes of hips and chins. Matt suddenly seems reluctant. Then someone on the balcony notices him.

'Matthew!' comes a feminine squeal.

He groans, just audibly, just loud enough for me to hear.

'Let's do it,' he says.

'Right.'

We walk up the pathway together, arm hairs touching.

'Matthew!' A suntanned Kiwi chick flicks away a half-smoked cigarette and throws herself at him. I stand back, look into the house. There are about twenty people all up, not few enough to be intimate, but not quite enough to be raucous. They're spread through the main living area and spill across the balcony. At one end of the balcony two Indonesian men flip fish and squid. There are only a couple of other Indonesians among the guests.

A man nearby steps forward, introduces himself as Dennis. At first glance he looks as though he should be attending an IT function in Perth. He wears thick-rimmed glasses, his hair is thinning black, and flakes of dandruff chase his neckline. But subverting the nine-to-five nerd image are the telltale signs of tropical wear: deltas of sun lines from the corners of his eyes, skinny protein-deprived wrists and an earth-coloured sarong that falls from his hips. I learn Dennis is in his forties and that he worked as an English teacher in Bandar Lampung where he met Meri, a local girl from Batu Batur. He's been here for seven years and teaches English a couple of days a week at one of the primary schools. For three months each year he goes back to Melbourne to work and save up enough money to support his family for the next year.

'That's my wife over there.' He points to a middle-aged woman in bulging jeans, chatting to another Indonesian woman.

'Do you reckon you'll stay here for a long time?' I ask. 'Don't you miss home?'

'Home? God no, Australia's not home! I can't get back here quick enough. When I first return to Aus after eight months here, I smile at people on the streets and chat to people on the train to work. It takes me a couple of weeks to readjust. Some of the looks I get, Jesus, you'd think I was a convicted paedophile or something.'

Without the tan and sarong, in a winter-subdued city at home, perhaps Dennis would seem like a man too eager for friendship, acceptance, belonging.

'No, this is my home now.'

I understand him; understand the discord of dual belonging. Sometimes I wish Mum had never let me move over to Bali to live with Dad when I was fifteen. Not that it was her fault, she didn't have much choice. It was either that or lose me completely. I was bored shitless at school and wagged every second day to go surfing or hang out at the skatepark. But fifteen is a terrible, impressionable age and that time with Dad shifted something within me. Friends who went on high school exchange, to Canada, to France, to Japan, say the same. They too are still pulled to these places, still feel like they have some kind of unfinished business, difficult to define.

Behind me, Matt's brushing off the Kiwi's giggles.

I'm curious as to how Dennis experiences Batu Batur, especially given the tensions. 'Matt said things have been a bit unsettled – that the locals haven't been that friendly toward the expats. Do you find that, given that your wife's from here?'

He looks at me keenly. 'It's interesting you ask. I think when you're a foreigner here, there's always some level of resentment. Because at the end of the day you're privileged. You've got money. It's as simple as that. But then just recently, I had four students pull out of my primary class and so I'm beginning to think there's something more to it.'

'What happened?'

'Many of the kids here don't get to high school, so it's not unusual to lose some early. But my wife thinks the kids' parents aren't happy their children are being taught by a bule. Probably Shane has a bit to answer for; he hasn't made us popular. Have you heard the latest?'

The man addresses his question to Matt and I turn so he can be included in our conversation. Matt's aftershave smells like lacquer and sandalwood.

'I haven't heard anything,' says Matt.

'This morning one of the mosques couldn't broadcast dawn prayer. They say Shane crept over to the mosque on his belly and cut off the electricity.'

Surely not, surely the rumour is too absurd, too dangerous to be true.

'Shane's a dickhead but I don't think he would be *that* stupid,' Matt says. 'It was probably just a power cut.'

'I tend to agree. But Meri heard that the cord to the loudspeaker had been severed.'

'It could've been backpackers. Or maybe rats.'

'Yes, that's possible.'

There's a pause, then Dennis asks, 'What brings you to Batu Batur? Are you travelling, on holiday?'

'Work.'

Matt's eyes have been prowling the crowd; now they snap back to me. I didn't *think* he heard me the other night at the bakso stand when I told him I'd just moved here. 'Oh yeah? What kind of work?'

I hesitate. 'I've got a job working for Shane.'

'Shane?' Dennis asks incredulously. '*Shane* Shane?'

'Yeah, well, good luck with that,' Matt adds, but his cynicism is tempered with concern. 'I reckon we should go inside and get a drink, eh? There's some stuff about Shane you probably should know. Will you excuse us, mate?'

He puts a firm hand on my shoulder blade and moves me inside to the drinks table. But there we become separated and the next couple of hours are a blur of conversations. My limbs liquefy, tongue loosens, heart rises to a giddy gorgeous state of drunk. I sweep around, meeting and mingling and feeling mad. An old German anthropologist and a fiery Dutchwoman own the house and have filled it with an eclectic range of artefacts: moth-wing lanterns, rare Indonesian textiles, gossiping Javanese puppets, skulls of monkeys and people. It's the kind of house I want one day, textured, a feast for the senses. And the guests are worldly, well read, entirely more thoughtful than the German and English backpackers I meet at work. Everyone seems to have a touch of the misfit about them, is searching for (or have found) a lifestyle, a belonging, they can't find at home.

At some point the Kiwi appears. 'So where did you meet Matthew?'

Not hi, what's your name, nice to meet you. The gin rises in me like a thin white whip.

'Actually I met him a couple of days ago. At a bakso stand. Have you guys known each other long?'

'What,' she rasps, blowing smoke over my shoulder, 'you eat that shit?'

'Yeah, I don't mind bakso.'

Someone once told me it was goats' balls in soup.

'Do you even know what's in the bakso here?'

'Goats' balls?'

'You're eating rats!' She's furious with my nonchalance. 'I bet Matt didn't eat any, bet he just watched!'

A few years ago in Bali a bunch of people got crook from rat poison. No-one could figure out how. Perhaps it was from the bakso. Inwardly I shudder. 'Oh well, it tasted okay to me,' I say.

Just as the Kiwi begins to respond, there's the rev and roar of motorbikes outside. It'd have to be close to midnight. I half turn my face toward one of the windows.

Gunshots.

The glass webs fast with cracks.

'Shit!' screams the Kiwi, diving to her belly.

I do the same. Outside, over the sound of engines, voices jeer, 'Bule! Eh bule!'

There's a hail of glass, another crack. I hold my breath, feel my lips against the grain of the wood, feel the grain of the wood against the pulse in my thumbs, think: play dead and keep your eyes shut, play dead and keep still. I send my mind to every part of my body, sure I've been shot, certain I'm in shock and just can't feel it yet. The sound of motorbikes recedes and is replaced by music, something Franz and Adalie chose for the party. Papuan, drums. No-one's speaking, no-one's screaming. I open an eye. The Kiwi opens an eye-shadowed eye. She meets my look of terror then slowly raises her head. When she doesn't get shot, I follow. The others stir, whisper, stir to their feet. I shuffle my legs. I haven't been hit, but there's a lake of glass on the inside of the window frames.

I scramble to my feet. Several large rocks rest among the broken glass. The gunshots were rocks, weighed in hands, hurled with hate.

Outside, there are the fresh track marks of motorbikes in the loamy earth, the skin-prickling presence of the jungle.

On the way home, Matt doesn't say a word.

14

I'm more expressive in Indonesian. My face comes alive in a way it doesn't need to when I'm rustling through the bored, lazy vowels of Aussie English. It's because I don't have the vocabulary to express everything I want and so my eyes and hands give colour and nuance to the things I can't properly explain. And because it's such a perfect bubbling language for gossip, it invites a layering of tones and gesture, expressions of complicity, mockery, incredulity. When I'm talking with Indonesians I don't mind being over the top to get my point across, but the presence of other bules always makes me feel uncomfortable, exaggerated.

'Did anyone see who did it?' Ibu Ayu asks.

'Nggak!'

The English guy throws me a look. The German girls ignore me, engrossed in a guidebook. The three of them are sprawled with relaxed indifference.

I lower my voice, say again no, no I don't think anyone saw who did it. Ibu Ayu's face glumly sweats.

'Hopefully it's not like the bombing in Jakarta,' she says finally. 'You see what it's like here. Almost empty. Barely any tourist. Especially not Australian. They go Thailand, Vietnam. Somewhere else. They think Indonesia too dangerous. It will be no good for my business if news gets out.'

'It was probably just kids.'

'But not kid from Batu Batur,' Ibu's tone is short. 'Definitely not kid from here.' She pushes back her chair. 'Lagi?' she asks, gesturing to my coffee.

'Sure.'

Ibu gets to her feet, takes an order for tea from the backpackers, and barks at Cahyati as she passes the kitchen.

I tilt my coffee glass on its side, watch the slide of sludge. I crashed as soon as Matt dropped me home, but my dreams were turbulent. Matt chased me with a gun. Josh cooked up a pan of gourmet ears, 'For bakso,' he said. Again and again through the night I woke sweaty and sick-mouthed and frantic. I steady the glass. It's going to be one of those days when even coffee can't shift the exhaustion.

I wonder what the rock throwing was about, whether it was deliberately linked to whoever sabotaged dawn prayer. Perhaps it was about a general dislike of the bules here, tourists included. We blow in, start our own businesses, pay the locals a pittance and then seal ourselves off in air-conditioned capsules, living above and beyond anything the average fisherman could ever hope for. It's pretty easy to see how this could be a cause of conflict. On top of this, most young Aussies who head to Bali for a holiday cut loose: end up doing things they wouldn't dare do at home. Just two weeks ago I was in a police chase for not wearing a helmet or shoes. The police waved me down but I'd had a few beers – okay, eight beers – and was feeling impulsive. Headphones on, rental bike throbbing between my thighs, throttle wrist taut, no, there was no way I was going to stop. They didn't catch me. All these factors could be a cause of conflict. Then again, perhaps there are bigger issues at play. The Bali bombings were only a couple of years ago. There was a bombing outside the Marriott Hotel last year. And in September, less than three months ago, a car bomb exploded outside the Australian Embassy in Jakarta. That's a pretty clear indication of animosity toward Westerners. Are the tensions spin-offs from this? Does Jemaah Islamiya, the Islamic militant group claiming responsibility for these bombings, have inroads, connections or influence in Batu Batur? Surely if they do they'd be more militant – would have homemade bombs or guns instead of rocks. I can't help but feel ashamed. To be stoned. To be told to fuck off with *rocks*!

This is not what I imagined in the month leading up to my flight. It was supposed to be a chance to run away – no, not to run away, but to take a breather from Josh, create a bit of distance. Instead, the sense of claustrophobia has followed me here. I've landed a job with a bloke who's gone troppo, who's loathed by locals and expats alike and apparently cuts the fingers off his staff. I probably should take off. I'm not bound by any contract, don't owe anything to Shane. It's ten days until I'm due to start and as far as I know, he's not aware I'm here. I can get on a bus and leave tomorrow, head back to Kuta, maybe find some work, spend my weekends shooting arak and dancing with a bunch of people I've met a hundred times before and never met, because along those narrow debauched lanes everything is always the same and always changed and the only thing that's certain is that it's easy.

But I don't want easy, don't want to go back to WA – I'm more open here, I laugh more, I feel more dangerously, boldly alive. And what if it's all just rumour, the stories about Shane? Before I make any decisions, I need to find out for myself. I'll head to his surf camp tomorrow.

Cahyati emerges from the kitchen, balancing a tall glass of coffee and three glasses of tea on a tray. She places the coffee in front of me (it's my fourth) then sets the teas down for the backpackers. The English guy snorts.

'What's this then? I asked for tea with milk.'

The girl stands there, tray trembling against her thighs and throws me a look of panic.

'Ada susu?' I ask the girl.

She nods and dashes back into the kitchen, returning a few moments later with a punctured can of condensed milk. She brushes a few ants from the side of the can and places it on the table. One of the German girls lifts the tin and turns it over in her hand, lower lip buckled in disgust.

'You've got to be kidding me,' says the English guy.

'Ja, stop complaining. At least is cheap to stay here,' says the German girl, placing the tin down.

'But I think Shane's Sumatran Oasis is a little bit cheaper maybe.' The other girl is poised over a *Lonely Planet* with a highlighter. 'It's a surf resort but it says there are dorms. We should go this afternoon.'

The English guy shrugs, sniffs his tea, then tosses it over the pond of waterlilies.

15

That afternoon I'm feeling nervous, edgy, bored. I can't focus on my book, can't think about anything much except the party last night. Even the memory of the bloke on the beach pales in comparison. I head off on another walk, not up the beach this time, no way, but into town.

The police station is about halfway in. Did Franz and Adalie report the incident? Have the police found out who was throwing rocks at the house? There's probably no harm in asking. The police are gathered in a damp courtyard sipping coffee from small plastic cups and smoking kreteks. When I call out a hello, one of them springs to his feet and leads me back to the reception desk inside. I tell him exactly what happened, then ask if they know who did it, if it was just kids mucking around, if this kind of thing happened often. The sides of his mouth drag down, as if by fishhooks. Idiot! It would've been better to soften the query with a permisi, a maaf, with some tactful circular conversation. So I slip fifty thousand rupiah across the counter, and say, 'Sorry Pak, perhaps this might help?' The officer looks at the fifty. Looks at me. Takes the fifty. Then tells me they don't know for sure but are investigating the incident.

I end up back at the bungalows with my feet up and *en passant* propped on a knee. After a while, the Frenchman ducks through the blue door. He places his board under a tree then waves for me to join him on his balcony. He doesn't look at me but stares at the ocean: it's insipid, the ribbed grey of old shells. There are no silhouettes.

It begins to rain.

After a while I say, 'Emile, have you been here in Indonesia for long?'

He looks startled as if from sleep. There are rockets of darkness in his eyes.

'I, no, not so long.'

'Where were you before Indo, have you been travelling for a while?'

'Oui. In a way. I've just come from Côte d'Ivoire. I am a photographer, a photojournalist. A few weeks ago nine French soldiers were killed by airplane. Now the situation is very –' he flicks his wrist, '– instable?'

'Unstable, yeah.'

The rain makes coral-like clicks on the roof.

'So will you work here?'

'No, here is for surf, maybe do some yoga, relax. Some horrible things I saw in that country.'

We fall back into silence.

16

It's one of those sweeping and sublime Indonesian dusks that presage disaster. The sky has the dark cracked texture of snake fruit except for just ahead, where it smoulders lava-like through the palm fronds. Men drag wooden carts over their shoulders, heads down, dusty as dokar horses. An old woman pedals a bicycle; her tiny granddaughter is tucked into a basket on the front. Eventually the buildings give way to rice fields; they run from the mountains all the way to the palm-fringed edge of the coast. Streams of wet light run in the folds between rice paddies.

Shane's is a long ride out of town. I didn't intend to arrive so late in the day but on the way I checked out several side roads leading to the coast to scope out the surf – one black-sand beachie had some form. Then I stopped for coffee alongside a waterfall foaming with detergent. Now at last, the turn-off to Shane's. The track's riddled with tree roots and runs for about fifty metres before opening on to a clearing. In the clearing, there are two men sitting on a log. One jumps to his feet.

'You looking for Mister Shane?'

'Yep.'

'No bag?'

'No bag.'

'Okay. My friend watch motorbike so no stealing.'

'Okay.'

'Two thousand rupiah.'

'Hey? I've got a job here, I start next week!'

'Does Mister Shane know you coming?'

'Yeah! Well, no. He doesn't know I'm coming today.'

He sticks out his hand. 'How about a cigarette?'

I pull a crumpled packet from the back pocket of my pants and offer them. The men inspect the pack and scoff. They're poor-men's cigarettes: filter-less, tar-full, smoked by becak riders, fishermen and kaki lima owners. Not the cigarettes smoked by employees of a bule.

'Two thousand rupiah,' the man says again. Grumbling, I fish out the money.

The man says something to his friend in a quick snicker of Lampung, then gestures for me to follow him. We cross a river on a swinging wooden bridge. It's only wide enough for one person. I trail my hand along the wire railing for balance.

Shane's Sumatran Oasis is just past the bridge. A dim bulb lights a back verandah. I'm at the door before I realise my guide is hanging back. I catch the crouching shine of his shins, the crumbling point of his cigarette.

'What's wrong?'

He shakes his head and waves his fingertips.

I turn and knock on the door. A muffled voice shouts for me to wait. There's the sound of vigorous footsteps. Shane swings open the screen door and for a moment, looking up at him, I'm stunned. From the stories I had imagined a mean Aussie bloke in his fifties or sixties with a beer gut, in a blue singlet, flaunting a spray of stars across his bicep. But Shane looks like he was once an ironman, an Olympic swimmer, Laird Hamilton's Aussie twin. His hair is surf-mag blond, thick not thinning, and it falls sideways over his eyes. His frame fills the door. He's looking at me with frank, warm interest. No way, I think. This *couldn't* be Shane. But there's also no way it could be a Swedish backpacker – the bloke has the stubble and sun lines and brazen don't-give-a-fuck look of an Aussie.

'Shane,' he says, sticking out his hand. 'Welcome.'

I shake his hand mutely.

He looks amused. Must happen to him all the time.

I follow him down a corridor plastered with posters of waves: Raglan, J-Bay, Mavericks, Padang Padang. At the end, a huge wooden balcony serves as an open-air living area. I expected the place would be like a shipwreck, full of sand and green with mould. Instead, it's modern, Western, and full of toys. There's a flat-screen television playing bits of last year's Quicksilver Pro, beanbags, padded board racks, low coffee tables stacked with surf magazines, a pool table, fussbal table, massage table, hammocks, a surf-check tower and a bar. Two-thirds of the balcony is shaded by a wooden roof, the other third is for the Bintang umbrellas, daybeds and deckchairs facing the surf. Off to the right, a corridor leads to rooms attached to the main building. Over the edge of the balcony, wedged between frangipanis and jasmine, are half a dozen bungalows.

'So, what can I do for you this evening? You lookin' for a room?' Shane asks.

'Not exactly …'

'Not exactly? How about some dinner then, or perhaps I can tempt you with a drink?'

'Actually, I'm your new manager. Penelope.'

'Ah, *nice*. Penny. I can call you that, right? I heard you were in town. Shall we grab a drink?'

He doesn't wait for me to answer, just strides across to the edge of the balcony and sets himself down in a chair.

The moon's rising through scissor-edged palms.

'Well?' he calls back to me.

'Sure.'

I'm wary. Wary of the charisma. Wary of the mismatch between the stories and the man.

'Kristi!' he calls out, sliding a kretek from the packet. 'Rokok?' he asks, nudging the packet toward me.

'Nggak.'

His eyes are close together and focused. 'So you speak a bit of Indo then.'

'Yeah. I lived here for a year when I was a kid.'

He shoots a flame from the lighter, takes a drag. 'Rotten habit,' he apologises, aspirating clove-warm smoke. 'Only in Indo.'

I laugh. He wouldn't be the first non-smoker to get hooked here. Even I'm partial to the occasional kretek.

A girl is suddenly next to us. She wears a pale cotton dress. Her shoulders are bare. She wouldn't be sixteen.

'Kristi, some drinks. What do you drink, love?' he asks me. 'Beer? Vodka?'

'You got gin?'

'Gin it is.'

The skin around the girl's eyes is black, as if pinched; the eyes themselves are as blank as unhatched eggs. She blinks.

'You heard our guest. A gin and tonic. And another beer for me. And please, Kristi, serve it properly this time, yeah?' When Kristi's out of earshot he says conspiratorially, 'You gotta watch 'em. If you're not careful they'll fuck everything up.'

'Mmm,' I murmur, in what I hope is a neutral tone. 'So you guys don't talk in Indo?'

'Nope. These people don't know I can speak their language. It's better that way.'

'Right.'

Beyond the trees I can hear the dark heave of the ocean. The sound is always more distinct at night. 'So you're pretty close to the surf here then?'

'Thirty-second walk to the water, fifteen-minute paddle to the best dry-season right-hander you'll find on mainland Sumatra.'

'What a spot!'

'Yeah, well, I guess like anywhere it has its challenges.' He glances over his shoulder. 'What's taking her so long?'

Five minutes in and already, inevitably, I'm baited to placate him. 'I'm sure she's not far,' I say quickly. Then, 'Do you still surf?'

'Be mad not to,' he says. 'But not as much as I used to. Had a couple of years on the tour when I was younger but ended up getting dropped. Blew it. Got distracted by beautiful women and drugs.'

He gives me a guileless grin and I find myself grinning back.

The girl is behind us again, waif-like, balancing a tray. She sets my glass on a low wicker table and fits Shane's beer to his hand.

'Thanks sweetheart.' He takes a long swing. 'I probably had more time in the water when I first moved here. But at the moment all my energy is going into keeping this place together. Keeping myself out of trouble.'

'What do you mean?'

'The locals here are fanatics. It's not chilled out, like Bali. I was seeing a girl for a while. She was from Bandar Lampung. A couple of days after I brought her here, a group of blokes from the mosque came round demanding to know who she was and where she was from and if I'd married her. They said no woman was to turn up and live with me unless she'd signed their book first.'

'What did you do?'

'Told 'em I'd do as I fucken well pleased!'

'So is it worth it then, staying here? You know, if the local crew aren't that friendly?'

Shane pulverises the kretek stump, adjusts a paw around his beer. 'When I first came here, to Batu Batur, I saw potential: great waves, cheap land, unbelievable location. I started with a losmen, extended that to some bungalows, then to this ... but it's been an uphill fucken battle. Do you know why?'

He's not interested in an answer. I put my mouth to the cool edge of my gin.

He gestures in the direction of Kristi. 'The locals,' he says in a low voice. 'They're either fanatics, lazy cunts or thieves. And you've got no idea how much money it costs. You think it's cheap to live here? Wrong. Something breaks, I gotta get it fixed, right? Even now, after livin' here for nearly ten years, they charge me twice the amount the locals pay!' The neck of his beer glistens. 'Then there's the issue of staffing. They're always complaining they don't get enough money. But why would I pay them any more? They hardly work as it is, the men especially. They spend most of the day squatting around smoking durries while the women do all the work. I only employ women now but, Christ, don't get me started on the local women!'

My steely silence gets him started; he mistakes it for attentiveness.

'Dolls to look at, the most beautiful women in the world. When I first came to Indonesia, to Yogyakarta to study, I rented a house opposite a local high school. When I wasn't at uni I sat out the front and watched the girls.'

He shifts in his seat. A giant hard-on swells against the fluoro polyester of his board shorts.

'Those legs, those firm little breasts, that hair!' His voice is husky. 'But all they want's your money. You're not a leso?'

'No,' I manage.

'Well, alright.'

'So if it's all that bad, why do you stay here?' I can't quite keep the challenge from my voice, can't quite keep my eyes from sliding back to his crotch.

Rain starts to fall. There's the gentle splash of rain in gin. The palms chafe, necks stretched tall in sacrifice, fronds ragged as the heads on effigies. He says nothing for a long while. Then, just at the point when it seems he's forgotten what I asked or has chosen to ignore me, he answers simply and without self-pity.

'Got nowhere else to go.'

I drain my gin.

'Kristi! More drinks!' The rain comes down heavier. 'Move ya chair.'

We resettle under a red and white Bintang umbrella. I wonder how I'm going to get home. Knowing my luck, I'll probably end up falling through one of the holes in the bridge, land in that slow-moving river churning with dysentery, typhoid, catfish fat on turds.

'You can stay tonight,' Shane says. 'I wouldn't be driving back in the dark if I were you. And this,' he gestures to my empty gin glass, 'this is all on me. I'm happy for the company. Can get pretty lonely out here this time of year. There's the occasional Euro backpacker who comes through, clutching their fucken *Lonely Planet*s and water bottles. All they do is complain about the bloody price. "Vair is the cheapest nasi campur?" I usually dump them in the dorm. The other crew are the Aussie surfers. Rough cunts. No conversational scope.'

I bite my tongue. 'If you don't mind me asking, what did you do at uni in Jogja?'

'Language, arts, the usual. One of those exchanges. Wasn't at uni much though. Spent a lot of time down around Pacitan surfing spots that weren't even on the map then. Outrageously heavy spots.'

Rain drops a pale screen in front of us. 'So, Shane, I mean, I haven't seen the rooms but from what I have seen the place looks great, it looks like it's being managed really well. Sorry if this sounds like a stupid question, but why did you hire me?'

'Jeez, I'm starting to wonder that,' Shane teases. 'Basically I need someone in here I can trust. Someone who's not gunna steal money from my guests or take weeks off because their uncle or great-grandmother's sick.'

Kristi arrives with our drinks.

'And I hired you because you were the only chick who applied. Didn't want some hungry young gun in here from the Goldy who'd end up competing with me and my guests for waves.'

Shane doesn't seem like a guy who would get on too well with other guys. He might have a few close mates, bonded by stupidity and youth, but it seems more likely that he'd stockpile women. If he had men around him it would be omega men, malleable and docile.

'So ... I know you said in the ad on the internet that the starting rate was –'

'Yeah, yeah,' Shane cuts me off. 'You want me to tell you about the benefits, right?'

'Right.' Already the starting rate was reasonable. More than reasonable, in fact, it was almost as much as I was getting paid at the backpackers and the pub combined. Given that the cost of living here was a tenth of the cost of living in Australia, I stood to save some serious money.

'Like I said in the email, you've got free accommodation. You can have any guest room of your choice – except for the bungalows. Free food. A lend of one of the motorbikes provided you pay for petrol and maintenance. I'll pay you every fortnight. And ...' he pauses, his trump card. 'If you stay for six months, I'll swing you an extra five grand.'

The glass nearly slips from my fingers. 'Are you for real?'

'I've had a high turnover of staff. I need someone steady who'll help lift the profile of this place in the community, who'll be on the internet putting ads on Wannasurf and Magicseaweed, do some guerrilla marketing, basically work their guts out. I want this place fully booked from May to September. You work your guts out, you stick around for six months, the bonus is yours.'

A cool five, plus free creative reign over the marketing side of things. That's a challenge. That's another trip. That's freedom.

Shane also doesn't seem anywhere near as bad as the stories would suggest. Matt probably badmouths him because he's an alpha male. Ibu Ayu and Bapak Joni are probably concerned because Shane's Sumatran Oasis is the only real competition. But although he certainly has problems respecting the local culture, I can't imagine him cutting the fingers off his staff.

My gin swallows an insect.

'Sounds unreal,' I say.

He responds with an almost imperceptible wince. His hand goes to his stomach, where once-chunky abs are slack from misuse.

'Well. Thanks for an awesome night. I'm looking forward to having you on board. But for now, I reckon it's time for me to hit the sack.' He puts down his beer. His hand trembles. 'Kris –' She's there before he squeezes out the last syllable.

Kristi draws him to his feet.

'Night, then.'

'Night.'

They walk together down the wooden corridor, past the guestrooms to the private arm of the resort. She doesn't come up to his armpit. His fingers slide down her spine, edge between her bum cheeks.

After a while, the girl emerges.

'Is he okay?' I ask her. 'Is he crook?'

'Nggak,' she says, ''gak begitu.' It's not like that.

'So what is it?'

Those blank eyes register distrust. She shrugs. 'He's not sick.' Then, with a haughtiness, a disdain she wouldn't dare display around Shane, she asks if I'm staying the night.

'Yeah, I guess so.'

She throws me the key to room twelve. It lands at my toes.

17

'Matt already come looking for you,' says Ibu Ayu. 'He say he come get you for the dawnie. I tell him you didn't come home last night, that you probably stay with some local boy.'

'You didn't!'

She gives me a wicked grin.

'You did!'

'Iya! Anyway, where you sleep last night?'

'Shane's,' I tell her.

'Kenapa kesana? Why you go there? You not happy here? You no like your bungalow? Still over a week, no, before you start?'

I laugh. 'Your bungalows are fine, Bu. I just went to Shane's to check the place out.'

'Ahh.' She changes the subject. 'Mau kopi?'

'Sure.' I pull up a seat and rest my forearms on the table. Anaemic sunlight leaks through the palm fronds. When I left Shane's earlier, the place was still damp with shadow. I couldn't find the girl, Kristi, and I wasn't keen to go poking around for Shane just to say goodbye. He wasn't at all like I expected; I was imagining a psychopath. Instead, he seemed reasonable enough, for a drunk.

Ibu brings out my glass of coffee and sits opposite me. She's silent for a while. Then all of a sudden she asks, 'So how come Matt looking for you here? Penny no have boyfriend in Australia?'

'Yeah, sort of. But we're having a break.'

Ibu looks perturbed. 'A break?' She shakes her head in incomprehension. 'Anyway, I don't know why this Matt always visiting you. He already have wife!'

'*What*?' I blurt. Then to cover my shock, 'Yeah of course. I know that. We're just mates. You're allowed to be just mates in Australia, it doesn't mean that ...' I trail off.

Satisfied she's warned me, she switches topic, asks me a question that makes me feel even more uncomfortable.

'So you already here one, maybe two week. What you think of Lampung people?'

Under the cap of her jilbab, her eyes are sharp as kitchen knives.

I think about the men in the bushes, the stalker on the beach. Similar things have happened to me in other parts of Indonesia, and in Mexico, Sri Lanka. Nothing ever really happened in Fiji. And the last time something happened in Indonesia, it wasn't a local at all, it was another traveller. It was the year after I finished high school and it was my first time back in Indo since I was a kid. I decided to go to Kalimantan, where there were rivers and gorillas and no chance of getting distracted from travel by the surf. On the flight from Denpasar to Balikpapan the only other bule was an American in his forties. We got chatting. I must have intrigued him, entranced him, naively. Do you want to get a taxi together to look for some accommodation? Sure. Cut the cost. Why not? We found a road of 'cheap' accommodation. Everything was overpriced. And at every intersection there were whores in bras and undies, jutting their hips, half-covering their faces with cloth. I had never seen this in Indonesia before; even in Kuta the girls were usually wearing dresses, were propped up at bars. It filled me with apprehension. In one losmen, the rooms glowed red from the lights of the Chinese brothel opposite;

cigarette butts were compressed onto the concrete floor and the bin was still overflowing. The staff didn't plan to clean it. Shit, let's step it up, said the American, so we did; agreed on sharing a room at a reasonable hotel. The American didn't speak Indonesian. *Tempat tidur terpisah*, I stressed more than once to the receptionist. We need a room with separate beds. *Please*, two beds. *Please*.

In the middle of the night the American tried to edge onto my single bed. I wasn't scared. I had my knife under my pillow. *Fuck off!* I unflicked it. That first knife was a beauty. A blade that could've halved a tongue. 'I thought you were masturbating,' he said. 'I thought you were masturbating over me.'

He slunk back to his bed.

I learnt a valuable lesson: never trust a bule just because you're also a bule in a foreign country.

Anyway, this incident was so much heavier than the man on the beach, so much heavier than the guys behind the trees. And situations like these are never necessarily indicative of the character of the people. So Lampung people … I think of my encounters at the markets, in the warungs and wartels. Push from my mind the fearful warnings of the expatriates, the rocks at Franz's the other night.

'They seem a little more guarded than people in other parts of Indonesia,' I say to Ibu, 'but on the whole, the people here are really friendly, much more friendly than in Australia!'

She's frowning, waiting for something more.

'I guess there's also the perception – and this is not just about orang Lampung but all through Indonesia – that the country is becoming more conservative.'

Ibu straightens her spine. 'How do you mean conservative?'

'Well,' I falter. I haven't really thought it through. 'Well, there are more women choosing to wear the jilbab than there were, say, fifty years ago. I've talked to Australian women who were travelling here in the sixties and seventies and had no problem wearing singlets and shorts. You wouldn't dare do that now. You definitely wouldn't do it here in Batu Batur.'

Ibu appears unconvinced. 'But what you mean when you say conservative?'

'More Islamic. More strict. More taat.'

Ibu shakes her head vehemently. 'Penny forgets. We've always chosen to dress like this. For Indonesian people, Islam is a symbol, not an ideology. Go to the village and you will see many traditional belief, traditional culture as well as Islam. A mix. But here, no, the problems have nothing to do with Islam.' She drops her voice. 'My father orang Madura, my mother orang Lampung. When I was small, my father warned me that Lampung people are very sneaky. In Madura if you have problem with some person you say okay, we fighting tomorrow three o'clock with kris knife. Fighting, fighting, no more problems. He die. But here it's different, ya? If a Lampung person doesn't like you, on a dark night with no moon he'll follow you home and arghh!' She makes a stabbing gesture with her hand. 'Knife in back. Finish.'

I place down my coffee. I've drunk too quickly and now my tongue is furry with burn. If orang Lampung would do this to orang Madura what would they do to Westerners who acted like cowboys? Then again, everyone gets tarred with generalisations. On my way here I had a night in Jakarta on Jalan Jaksa. Nigerians sailed past in immaculate white pants. Old bules with gravity-stricken guts were led quietly by pretty Sundanese girls. Backpackers with towering old-fashioned rucksacks and dirty clothes clutched brand new laptop cases. Inevitably, I ended up in a bar. Got yarning with an American bloke and a Javanese madam who'd worked in Bali for years. When they learnt I was Australian, their mouths became chisels. The madam told me of the appalling way Aussie blokes treated Indo women on hotel beds in Kuta. About how slovenly and stingy and dumb we were. 'And all you damn Aussies,' concluded the American, 'you all act as if you own the place!'

Ibu Ayu's generalisations remind me of this. Half-truths.

Mmm. So the Lampungese are quick-tempered.

And Matt's got a wife.

18

The wartel owner doesn't acknowledge me when I duck through the doorway and into his shop. He's reading a paper behind his bench.

'Can I use the phone?'

He doesn't look up.

'Thanks.' Perhaps his wife is giving him a hard time.

Josh picks up the extension straight away.

'Penny!' he says, 'Long time no hear! How've you been?'

That's the thing about Josh. He gets over things fast.

I try to match his brightness. 'Pretty good! I met my new boss yesterday. There's a five grand bonus if I stay six months. And guess what? I'm going surfing in the next few days!'

There's that three-second pause that makes spontaneous conversation impossible on long-distance calls. It's just long enough to start thinking about something else before the other person has a chance to respond.

'That's great,' he says, but he sounds distracted.

'So what have you been up to?'

'Actually, I've just hired ten new staff under the age of thirty. They come on board at the start of the week.'

'That's wonderful.' Bankrolled by his parents, Josh started a graphic design business as a seventeen year old that has grown to become the biggest in Perth. When we first met, I was unbelievably attracted to his mind, to his creativity, to the way he bounced ideas off me, nightly. And to the sex. What they say is true – sex with older men can be very, very satisfying.

'I got the new contract with that mining company EXO,' he continues. 'We've been hired to do all their rebranding. It's probably good timing that you're away now, I'm going to be flat out over the next few months.'

'Awesome!'

'Yeah, we're all heading off early for drinks.'

I don't answer.

'Penny, are you there?'

'Yeah.'

'You've gone all weird on me. Is something wrong?'

'Nah, it's just … I wish I could be there with you.'

I'm jealous. Unreasonably. Of that receptionist. Of the new, and probably hot, young staff.

'Well you could be, if you wanted.'

There's a three-second pause.

He continues, 'So have you decided? Do you reckon you'll stay away six months?'

'I …' Another six seconds untick. There's no way I'll land something like what Shane's offering back in Perth. Not without a degree, hotel school, more experience.

There's smothered voices at the other end.

'Ah, Josh? Are you still there?'

More voices, then he's back on the line.

'Sorry Pen, I've gotta go. Give us a call when you know what you're doing. And can you please, *please* sort yourself out with a mobile phone?'

I pay the wartel owner. Slump in the doorway and look out over the street. The night before I left, when Josh finally came to bed, cheeks now dry, he held me to him. It was as if he sensed the distance in my heart and was trying to will me back, through skin.

'What will you miss about me?' I asked, mouth muffled against his chest.

He was quiet a long while, then said, close to my ear, 'I'll miss the way you're interested in everything, the way you ask questions of anyone without worrying what they think. I'll miss the way you think about some things much more deeply than you let on, but then how with other things, things that are common sense to most people, you're completely oblivious to.'

'And what won't you miss?' I asked, turning, so my back was to him.

His arms locked around my chest. My lips touched one of his slender fingers. He didn't answer.

19

Twenty minutes later I'm flat on my back with my pants around my ankles. The bed looks like a hospital stretcher from WW2. The girls haven't bothered to put down a clean towel and it's glossy with filth. As soon as they roll out a dirty, bubbling wax pot on pram wheels, I sense trouble.

I should leave. But beauty salons are great places for gossip.

'Hello Missus! Where you from? Are you married? How long you in Batu Batur?'

I answer as best I can, feeling a blistering lick of wax across my pelvis.

'Mister Shane? You're going to be working for Mister Shane?' one of them asks incredulously.

A bandage rips. The girls quickly press their fingers against my skin to ease the pain.

'You're not scared?' asks the first girl, switching to Indonesian.

'Should I be?' At the moment, I think I'm more scared about getting third-degree burns.

'It's just a rumour,' says the second girl.

'Oh ya?' challenges the first.

'What's just a rumour?' I ask.

'About Shane chopping the fingers off one of his maids. I know the truth.'

Another slap of wax.

'My cousin knows Yuliana. She told me Yuliana worked in

Saudi Arabia as a maid for two years. That's where it happened. Her boss cut off her fingers because he thought she'd been stealing. It happens all the time.'

She whips off the bandage.

No soothing fingers this time.

'So why are people saying Shane did it?'

'Ya, people don't like Shane. They'll say anything to get rid of him.'

I hobble out forty minutes later after declining the offer of a 'crackwax', nearly hairless, with burns boxing in my vagina. Relieved as I am by this counter-rumour, there's no way I'll be going back to find out more.

20

At the bungalows Cahyati passes me a folded square of paper.

It reads: *Seeya at 6.*

'Matt?'

Cahyati nods.

I sit next to her on the top step leading up to the dining deck and follow her gaze. She's watching the Frenchman. He's set up a couple of speakers on his balcony and is positioned on a sarong in an ambitious, physics-defying yoga posture. His legs are around his neck. And he has an audience. On the other side of the fence several men straddle motorbikes. One of the men has perched a toddler between the handlebars. The toddler is wailing in alarm – the Frenchman's probably the first bule it's seen. The men chat and pass around a cigarette and no-one shows any signs of moving.

I haven't spoken to Emile since that afternoon on his balcony when he told me he had just come from snapping photos in Côte d'Ivoire. I wonder if his reticence, his inwardness, is because of something he saw.

'Have you been here for long?' I ask Cahyati in Indonesian.

'Maybe a month. My family are still in the village.'

'Do you like it?'

'Yeah …' she says unconvincingly. Then after a moment she asks, 'Have you ever been to Bali?'

'I used to live there.'

Above us a rat disturbs the rafters, looses a faint rain of dust and dead insects.

She lifts her face, but her shoulders remain hunched over. 'Is there much work there? Like cleaning work, restaurant work?'

'Sure. I mean usually it gets busy around May through until August. It's pretty quiet at the moment, especially after the bombings in Jakarta. But Christmas isn't too far away, and so a fair few tourists will start to come through after that. Why, are you thinking you might head over?'

'Maybe. Maybe if I can save enough money for the bus.'

That would be one hell of a bus trip. 'Kasihtahu aja, ya, kalau mau bantuan,' I say flippantly. Let me know if I can help out.

If she's serious, it's unlikely her family will let her go. But then again, there's a surprising mix of young people in Kuta. It's one of the things that makes the place so exciting, the fact that there's this constant influx of young people from all over the archipelago: all full of dreams, all living in shared accommodation, all falling in love, falling out of love, getting drunk, learning English, sending home money to their families. Each group tends to stick together – the guys and girls from Lombok hang out, the crew from Flores share accommodation, the soccer games on Kuta Beach at dusk are determined by island – the Sumatrans will be playing one game, but in the next game down, it'll be boys from Sulawesi.

'How old are you?' I ask curiously.

'Seventeen.'

'Are you still at school?'

'No, I left when I was fourteen.'

'Ahh. So do you have a boyfriend?'

She gives me a cheeky, spirited smile and her face transforms. 'Nggak!' she lies.

'Masak! Pacarmu masih di kampung, ya?' Yeah, right! He's

still in the village, isn't he?

She just smiles again. I learn that Ibu won't let her go into town unaccompanied and that she has no friends here. She's not keen to come surfing with Matt and me in the morning – she can't swim and surfing isn't something she wants to try. She does like soccer though; maybe, if I liked, we could go and watch the game tomorrow evening at dusk?

'I'd love that!' I tell her.

She squeezes my hand in excitement.

'But Ibu will be cool with it, with you taking the afternoon off?'

She drops my hand. 'Probably,' she says.

21

I wake with the call to prayer and lie still, listening to the timber-sigh of the bungalow, the black roar of surf over the reef. The waves here are nothing like the freezing, shark-chopped slabs in Albany. Indo's a warm-water playground of perfectly sculpted reefs that trap and jack perfectly groomed waves. Even so, I hope Matt won't coax me out if it's too big. It's been a long time and I don't want to have to do the paddle of shame back in.

I swing my legs out of bed and find the light switch.

Half an hour later I'm hunched behind Matt on his motorbike, clutching a board under each arm and holding on to him with my knees and thighs. It's cold; my cheeks and fingers and eyes smart. Matt's wearing a hoody, jeans and beanie. Before we left, he said, 'You might wanna get a jumper, eh.' I laughed and replied, 'Nah, I'll be right.' Stupid, stupid! I press my forehead against his back, imagining my hands wrapped around a glass of black coffee instead of cold fibreglass.

It happens every trip, an acute pang of First World guilt. We're flying along narrow roads, passing women and men whose bodies are halved over new rice, passing old women buckled under bundles of sticks and yet here *we* are, off to surf, off to play and play and play, for *months* if we want, while these farmers work their guts out, for our coffee, for our rice.

By the time we get there the sun's just coming up. We're south of Batu Batur, over the river and around to the southern end of the next bay. I climb off, arms aching, careful not to bump the boards together. Matt parks the bike under a palm. He warned me not to bring anything of value, not to bring anything.

'They're pretty desperate here. I've even had sunscreen stolen. Fuck knows why, they don't even use sunscreen!'

'Can't you lock stuff in the bike?'

'Yeah, but the seats are easy to lift. Year and a half ago some American blokes had their bikes stolen from this spot.'

We have turned down a grass track and ridden for ages. There are no people around, only a few cows with rusty, squared-off bells. It'd be a bitch to have to walk back to the main road.

'Yeah, it's not like in Aus where you chuck your key under the wheel of your car. It takes a bit more planning. But it's worth it.'

We walk clear of the palms. The ocean is the powder blue of mid-winter daydreams. About a hundred metres out, a right-hand wave peels flawless and glassy into a wide channel. The inside section is sucking up and barrelling, but further over on the shoulder there's a second, more mellow take-off point, where the wave slows, but doesn't stall – perfect for me! It peels almost all the way to the shore. There's no-one on it. I startle Matt with a whoop and a clap and sprint back to the boards. It's been pretty much two years since Fiji, two years since I've been out for a proper wave. Giddy, champagne-light bubbles rise in my chest, that promise of adrenaline.

'Wow, Pen, careful!' Matt's grinning, shaking his head at my excitement.

I admire his board, a green twin-fin fish with hand-sketched designs across the deck. Then I look again, now dubious, at the board I picked for myself. It was the best of a bad bunch of rentals from Ibu Ayu's, a mini-mal with a rounded nose and tail. Looking at the sunken fibreglass around the nose and fins, I find myself hoping it will float. Only one way to find out. I strip down to my bikini, scrunch my t-shirt and shorts under a bush, scribble on some wax and zinc and run to the edge of the ocean.

I remember another time, years ago, going for a surf with a guy I had a crush on. Stupidly, I fastened my leg-rope where we'd left our towels, way up on the sand. Then I ran down the sloping bank to the surf, leg-rope bouncing against my calf. Just as my toes were about to touch the water, I tripped on my leg-rope and flew face-first onto the sand bar. I grazed the end off my nose.

The bloke never asked me to go for a wave again.

This morning I'm more careful. I strap my leggy above my right ankle, wade out until the water rings my waist, then balance on the board and begin to paddle. Slow, steady strokes. My arms remembering. Matt soon catches up and we paddle out together. We move away from the channel and circle in behind the break. Coral opens out beneath us, dusty with salt and still-dark – though every now and then fish flicker past, violet, teal, lemon.

The sun splits knife-thin above the volcanoes.

Matt doesn't spend any time teabagging: he turns and paddles hard into the first set wave, swooping down the face. White fans of spray open and fall from the back of the wave. I'm not so game. I let the other four set waves go, wondering where my take-off point should be and how far the coral is below the soles of my feet. Matt catches another couple then paddles over.

'What's goin' on? You alright?'

'Yep.' A wave darkens to my right, a smaller one. I swing my board around and start to paddle. The wave picks the board up but as I try to jump, my feet scramble and the wave sucks and chucks me over the falls. I come up, coughing and embarrassed. Damn, Penny, come on. You used to be heaps better than this. You never would have missed such an easy take-off! I grit my teeth, paddle back toward the channel, then let it drift me behind the break again. I'm determined not to stuff up the next wave, determined that by the end of the session I'll be taking off on the inside and surfing with at least a fraction of the grace I used to have.

A couple more stuff-ups, a couple of shin-grazes on the coral, then it starts coming back. I've always enjoyed riding longer boards and by the end of the session I'm matching Matt wave for wave. I remember that graceful, swooping pattern: how to drop into an arcing bottom turn, angle the board toward the lip of the wave, then swing again when reaching the top, throwing spray from the tail. I remember how, when a wave fattens out, to move my hips, just slightly, to give me more speed; how to dance my feet to make the most of every glassy section, how to crouch low and drag my fingertips through the fish-flashing wall when the wave sucks over. I also remember how paddle-fitness is half of surfing and realise I'm seriously out of shape. No more kretek cigarettes or deep-fried bananas.

At last, Matt holds up his finger. One more. He positions himself, takes off, pulls into the curl of the inside section. Then he stretches out, graceful but with a tenseness, an expectancy; he's planning his next turn and from there everything flows, his body dark and fluid, tensing and relaxing, his board quick and loose and responsive beneath his feet. I turn and paddle for the wave after, jumping to my feet and chasing my reflection to the shore.

On the way home I grin and whoop and Matt keeps looking over his shoulder to check I haven't fallen off the back of the motorbike. If we'd taken separate bikes we could be racing each other, swinging around potholes, overtaking trucks, flying low around corners and scattering chooks. There's the taste of salt on my lips, my hair crackles with it; I can't believe I've forgotten what it feels like to surf. When I first moved to

Perth, I gave it a break. Sometimes Scarborough got surf, but it wasn't like Indo, or Fiji, or Albany. You either had to live it, or block it out completely – all or nothing. Sometimes, bored at the backpackers, I'd find myself indulging in surf porn, flicking through photos of Samoa, Nicaragua, the Maldives and Japan. Wondering if I should take off again, become a full-time surf gypsy.

And then I met Josh. He didn't surf.

Gradually, the ocean loosened her grip. But not really.

'You wanna drink?' Matt asks over his shoulder.

'For sure!' We skid to a stop beside a plastic awning-covered warung at the side of the road.

'Watch the knalpot,' he warns.

The inside of my right calf is shadowed with old, planet-shaped burns.

I swing off the opposite side to the exhaust pipe. We lay the boards wax-down on the grass and then sit at a long wooden table. On the table is a pot of sambal, a plastic container of spoons and forks and a dish of red and green chilli. We're the only customers.

'They do the best smoothies in Batu Batur.'

'That's quite the call!'

'They're quite the smoothies. You hungry?'

Not just hungry, but that intense, post-surfing-in-Indo hunger, where you eat yourself to bursting then fall asleep, skin rocking against your bones.

We order banana and mango smoothies, plates of fried rice. We don't speak until the plates are polished, the glasses drained. Matt crosses his legs, leans back and lights a kretek. He's watching me, sideways, slyly, from behind the smoke of his cigarette. Today his eyes are a confident, coral green.

Now that we're sitting down together, I want to come straight out and grill him about this wife of his but I don't get the chance, he's asking, 'So have you had a chance to check out Shane's?'

It takes me a moment to respond – his eyes have immobilised me. 'Right, yeah. Shane's. I went a couple of days ago. Just for a night.'

'And?'

'And … I don't think he's gunna be that easy to work for, but then, he doesn't seem like the psychopath Ibu Ayu describes.'

Matt taps loose a crown of ash.

I continue, 'Maybe he's come to the realisation that he's not always that good front of house and that he needs someone to kick his marketing up a gear. It's the wet season at the moment, so it's pretty quiet, but I guess he's hoping that by July his numbers will have really jumped. He's promised me an extra five grand on top of the wage if I stay for six months. I'm thinking I'll stick it out. I can't go back to WA. Not yet.'

'Just between the two of us, Pen, I don't think Shane'll still be here in six months. I wanted to talk to you about this at the party the other night. There's some guys in town who really have it in for him. Things are gunna come to a head in the next week or two, I'll put money on it.'

'But Joni told me that he's paying bribes to the police for protection. Doesn't that count for anything?'

'Yes and no. He might be paying bribes to the police, but you've lived in Bali, you know how corrupt they are. Do you reckon the fishermen whose beach he's on are getting a cut? Do you reckon the other business owners like Bapak Joni are happy about the competition? The thing is, Pen, we're all just hanging on here by the skin of our teeth.' Matt stabs his kretek into an ashtray.

'But to have a business here, you have to have a partner, right? Like, as a bule, the land has to be in the name of an Indo?'

Matt nods, 'Yeah, there's a couple of ways to go about it. I don't know what Shane's situation is, but I imagine it's in the name of a girlfriend, or ex-girlfriend, or ex-wife, something like that.'

'But surely if it were an ex-missus she'd be demanding the place for herself, for the cash?'

The waitress approaches our table. Matt stacks our plates, spoons and forks and hands them to her.

'Yeah, who knows,' he says, picking up a green chilli from the condiments bowl and popping it in his mouth. There's a twinkle, a dare in his eyes.

I'm impressed. The local kids pop chillies as if they're lollies but I've never seen a bule go them whole. I reach over and take one myself, but go slow, in tiny nibbles.

'So how did Shane seem to you? Like, health-wise?'

What a strange question to ask. 'He got crook toward the end of the night. He'd probably been on the piss since lunch.'

'Breakfast.'

'Yeah, well he's a pretty big bloke. I imagine it would take a fair bit of beer to get him tanked.'

We're no longer alone. A few men are bent over bowls of fried rice and noodles. Between spoonfuls they watch us with cheerless, equivocal eyes. There's none of the usual chat you get in warungs, none of the usual questions, the usual friendly banter.

I turn back to Matt. 'So do they know who threw the rocks at the party?'

Matt finds my toes with his toes under the table. A moth hatches in my throat, in my belly, between my thighs. 'We shouldn't talk about this here,' he says quietly, and his eyes move over my shoulder, then back to my face. 'You ready?' His toes shift away.

I nod. 'So when do you have to work again?'

'Next week,' he says as he stands.

Fifteen minutes later we're back at the bungalows.

'Do you want to come up for a …' It's too early for beer. Idiot! I can feel the colour lift in my cheeks and I tighten my fingers around my board.

'For a what?' he teases. 'Nah, it's cool, Pen, I gotta go. But I'll drop round tomorrow arvo for a drink. Hey, on a serious note. You should really think twice about taking up this position with Shane. In fact, you should leave Batu Batur. Get out of here. You don't owe Shane anything.'

22

The dead hours. Surf sore. Full of conflict and lust. For Matt. I wet the tip of my finger with my tongue then lift out my undies and gently brush tingles into my clit. I imagined it's the tip of Matt's tongue, working me gently, slowly. I imagine my fingers meshed in his bright hair, imagine him lapping me while his hands find and trail the sensitive hollows of my back. We're on a beach at sunset, we're in his village shack, we're locked under a tree; he's sinking his whole mouth around me, sinking deep his hard white teeth. I imagine reaching that point where the moans are no longer just expressions of gratitude but well up and cascade and tumble over each other of their own volition, rising out of some primal part of me, uncontrollable, implacable, with a tone that's so foreign, until the whole dark world behind my eyelids implodes, explodes.

I roll over onto my side. Feel guilty. See Josh, sobbing, on the edge of the bathtub.

23

That evening I head to the other side of town with Cahyati to watch the soccer. If she thinks I should be worried for my safety in Batu Batur, then she never lets on. By the time we get to the field the game is already in full swing. Half of the football ground has been drummed to a swamp by boots and the forked prints of toes. The boys skid and yowl and sweat their way up and down the field. A crowd cheers them on – Cahyati tells me it's the semifinal between Batu Batur and Bengkulu.

'So which one is he?' I ask.

She giggles behind her hand and pulls me to a warung overlooking the field. She orders two iced coconut drinks but when I push some rupiah toward her she shakes her head and clenches her fists. We stir our drinks and watch the game. It's hard to tell which team is which, but I'm infected by the enthusiasm of the crowd, the community-feel on the sidelines: toddlers tear-arse through the mud, teenagers with diagonal pop-star fringes stand in awkward groups, women nurse babies. Alongside the main field something else has started up. A bunch of primary school–aged girls are kicking a ball between themselves, making intimations toward a game of their own.

'They shouldn't be playing soccer.' Cahyati has followed my gaze to the girls.

'But they're just kids.'

'Girls don't play soccer.' Her voice is surprisingly firm.

We turn our attention back to the main game. There's a penalty kick, 'For Bengkulu,' Cahyati tells me. The crowd's shouting, waving fists, revved up on sugary coffee and localism. The kick flies wide and the shouting becomes cheers, the volume trebles. Then Cahyati tugs at my sleeve. 'Look.'

A man in white is striding toward the girls.

'Come on, let's see what he says.' She pulls me from the warung and across the grass toward the girls. Other people have gathered around, curious. By the time we're in earshot, the girls are all looking at their feet and the soccer ball has been dribbled off by a boy. The man's tone is unbearably patronising.

'Who is he?' I whisper.

'Abd al Hakim. The head of the big mosque, the one near the market.'

The man has the distinctive hooked nose of an Arab and stands a head taller than me. The rest of his features are Indonesian; he's probably from Aceh. There's something uncomfortably shrewd in his long, distinct face. He senses he's under scrutiny.

'Ah!' he says. 'Bule! Did you persuade these girls to play?'

Cahyati's nearly breaking my fingers with her grip but luckily, at that moment, there's a roar from the crowd and the man's attention swings. Batu Batur has won. She pulls me away toward the sideline and one of the players, number seven, glances our way, just briefly. Cahyati's mouth twitches into a wafer of a smile, then her face becomes impassive again.

We get back to Ibu Ayu's on dusk. Cahyati slips into the laundry to catch up on the chores she's missed and I head straight to my bungalow to put on mozzie repellent – dawn and dusk are the worst times for mozzies and I'm not keen to start a six month stint with malaria shivering through my blood.

Ibu Ayu sees us return. She's sitting at one of the tables on the dining deck, slowly fanning herself with a yellow flap of newspaper.

Later that night, on the cusp of sleep, I hear her cursing Cahyati for something, for some stupid thing that Cahyati's forgotten to do.

24

It's just after 4am and the gas lamps of the morning market wink warm as fireflies. Here in Indo, I never get that feeling I'm the only person alive. If you want to head out for a snack and a chat at 11pm, at 2am, at 4am, there's always somewhere open, there are always people around.

As a teenager in Kuta I often woke up before dawn, when the nightclubs locked the tills and drunk Aussies swung their legs over rental bikes and went screaming and careening through the alleys. If I couldn't get back to sleep I strapped my surfboard to my bike, hit a morning market for a hot bowl of bakso, stuffed fat parcels of sticky rice into my pockets and then headed north to Canggu, or east to Serangan, or south to the Bukit Peninsula: reckless, restless, suntanned and scab-kneed.

Up ahead there's a kaki lima selling deep-fried banana.

'Pagi Bu,' I greet the kaki lima owner, 'boleh minta pisang goreng?'

'How much do you want?' she replies.

'Dua ribu.'

The woman looks at me and firms her mouth. 'We only sell five thousand rupiah worth of pisang goreng.'

'You don't sell two thousand worth?'

Ibu Ayu paid two thousand rupiah only a few days earlier.

The woman shakes her head and goes back to flipping the bananas.

A moment later, a man approaches with his son and orders two thousand rupiah worth of pisang goreng. The woman spoons it into a white paper bag.

I turn away.

Batu Batur's market is a typical honeycomb of alleys, wooden display racks and plastic awning. Not big enough to get lost in but big enough to explore. This morning it seems to be crawling with beggars, touts and thieves. I move my bag around to my chest and clutch it, edging my way between the narrow stalls. Women argue over the price of spice, tongues like the tails of stingrays, hands deftly guarding a cornucopia of old cloves, vanilla beans, saffron and nutmeg. Slabs of raw beef, chicken and fish are lined up on the concrete floor and seasoned with cigarette ash and flies.

Among the stalls of clothing there's a group of women selling textiles, including the woman whose weavings I looked at a few days ago. When they see me their chat becomes frenzied and one woman sings out, 'Hello Mister, hello Mister! You looking, looking, okay?' The others quickly join her, singing, 'Duduk, duduk!' and so I sit with them, cross-legged. Someone brings me a steaming cup of black coffee. Someone else asks if I'd like a chair. As I look through the pieces I talk to the women about their families, their children, their husbands, their goats. They tell me they caught a bus to Batu Batur from the mountains this morning.

'What time?'

'Pagi pagi benar!'

'How early is very early?'

'Three thirty this morning. We left at three thirty,' they tell me.

'No way!'

I pretend to faint with tiredness and they slap my arms and laugh. It's so different to shopping in Australia; I love the pace of it, love the laughter, love how when I offer a price, the women roll their eyes and wail too low! too low! we'll go broke! and then they change the subject. We go back to talking about men or goats. Then after a while one of the women offers another price, a little lower than the last, and I shriek, too expensive! kok mahal? and the whole thing starts again.

I think about grocery shopping in Australia. The plethora of choice. The sterility. The waxy, tasteless fruit. The indifferent or surly or bored staff on the checkouts, blowing their noses, checking their watches. Sitting with these women yarning, arguing and bartering, I feel so much more comfortable, so much more alive!

After another half-hour of riotous laughter and lascivious yarns – through which I assemble a romantic history of their village – I buy two pieces. As money changes hands, they invite me to the mountains to meet their children and their husbands and their goats. I thank them, but Matt's swinging past this afternoon and I don't want to miss him.

God I'm a disgrace!

'Maybe in a couple of days.'

'Of course! Anytime! You are welcome, Mister, you are welcome.'

While I felt safe and shielded by the warm gossip of the women, on my way out I have an unnerving feeling that I'm being followed. It's not uncommon for bules to be shadowed through markets by thieves – the Pasar Badung in Denpasar is notorious for its hard-eyed 'guides' – but although I look over my shoulder a few times, there doesn't seem to be anyone lurking behind the scaly mounds of snake fruit.

Out on the main street two young men in skullcaps lean loose-limbed over a motorbike. One of the young men holds a monkey on a chain. The monkey is barely recognisable – it wears an obscene and eyeless mask. Music trickles from a box and the monkey strains against its chain in a rhythmless desperate dance. A child claps. The monkey dances. Then the men see me and make a hissing noise between their teeth and tongues. Lust and violence in equal parts. I keep walking.

25

I borrow a bucket from Ibu Ayu and head to the kamar mandi to wash my clothes. The bathroom here is communal and about fifty metres from my bungalow. There's something grounding in the rhythm of scrubbing clothes. It's the same rhythm you find when you're kneading dough, or working with earth or clay.

I'm just about finished when I hear a man's voice outside the bathroom.

'A week. Maybe ten days. No more.'

I can't quite place it. It's quietly authoritative; almost patronising, suggestive of someone who is used to having his orders obeyed.

'That's not enough, we need longer.' This time it's Bapak Joni, his tone gently persuading. 'It won't happen overnight. They say he's already sick. At least this way the police won't get involved. A little more time and then we won't need to –'

'We don't have more time,' the man says.

Bapak Joni sighs.

Their footsteps fade.

Thunder jars above the coconut trees. Shadows, sticky as tar, spread beneath palm and awning. I gather my wet clothes and run for my bungalow before the rain. Hopefully the afternoon will bring wind or muggy sunshine so my clothes will dry.

Just as the rain starts to lash down over the thatch, it occurs to me who the other voice might belong to. I'm not certain, won't put money on it, but it sounded like Abd al Hakim, the Arab-Indo looking guy from the soccer game.

26

There's a restless energy in Matt's movements. He leans over the balcony rail, face turned toward the evening ocean-roar, hands clenching and unclenching in excitement.

'You alright?'

He doesn't answer, just grins.

'Get any waves today?'

'Yeah.' There's a manic junky gleam in his pupils. It's obvious he's been in the water all day: the wrinkles at the corners of his eyes have whitened against his flushed, dark skin like the roots of tiny plants in soil. I want to brush them with my fingertips, to kiss them.

'Whereabouts?'

He laughs and puts a finger to his lips.

I roll my eyes – surfers are always so precious about their secret spots! 'Do you want a beer?'

'Sure.' He slews into the seat next to me and stretches out his legs.

A twisting, salty breeze jostles my bras and undies. They hang above us on a makeshift clothesline. I hope nothing falls on Matt's head.

His next question makes me forget the undies.

'So I've been meanin' to ask ya.'

'Mmm?'

'You got a bloke back home?'

I take a panicked sip of my beer and keep my gaze fixed straight ahead. On the lamp. On the zeppelin-blur of burning insects. Mumble, 'Sort of. We're having a break.' Then quickly, 'And you? You got a missus at home? Wait – you're married, right?'

'Yeah …' he draws it out, perhaps to give himself more time to think.

'I've got a missus at home,' he says at last. 'We're not married. When she was over here I told everyone we were, just makes it a bit easier, bit more culturally acceptable.'

'Oh yeah. So how long's it been since you've seen her?'

'Nearly eight months. She reckons if I don't come home by the end of the month it's off.'

'She doesn't want to live here?'

He rolls the bottle between his palms. 'Nah, not really, eh. When she was here we were living at my place in the village. It's pretty rustic. Sporadic electricity, water from the well. I'm away heaps with work and then when I'm back, I'm usually away surfing. So Gemma had a lot of time by herself, which she doesn't handle very well. She didn't really try to learn any Bahasa, so she couldn't communicate with our neighbours, and she reckoned she had nothing in common with any of the expats – hated Marika, the Kiwi chick you met the other night.'

The corners of my mouth twitch into a smile. I can understand that. Marika certainly did her best to rub me up the wrong way and clearly has a thing for Matt.

'Then I think it was just a lot of hassle, you know, being a chick. With the local blokes. One time I was out surfing and I left Gem on the beach. I paddled out and once I was out there, checked to make sure everything was cool. There was a bunch of guys circling her. One minute – empty beach at the edge of the jungle. Next minute, eleven guys.'

I pick at the edge of my beer label. 'That's hectic. What happened?'

'I was shitting myself. I got a wave straight in and threw out some chat, greased some palms and it was all cool. But if I hadn't been there, there would have been some serious trouble.'

The breeze tongues wet and hot through the palms.

'So, to cut a long story short, she got crook with malaria. I was away, surfing this island off Sumba with three mad cunts, the Scar Reef Boys: an American, a Kiwi and an Aussie. Scored some epic, heart-stopping waves. Fuck!' His eyes glaze a moment with the memory. 'Anyway, by the time I got back Gemma had pissed off.'

If I hadn't been a surfer, I would've thought he was an arsehole. Wouldn't have understood the obsession, that hunt for the perfect moment, for those few brief seconds crouched under the curl of the wave, heart in mouth.

It rips countless relationships apart.

'You don't want to be based in Bali instead and just fly back here for work?'

Matt frowns, crosses his legs the other way. 'Nah. I don't surf in Bali anymore. It's an absolute circus. On my weeks off, this is where I want to be.' He looks warily over at the Frenchman's bungalow and lowers his voice. 'An hour and a half from Shane's, toward Padang, there's this series of reefs. You gotta walk off the road and through the rice paddies to get to it. It's set up like a reverse Ulus, only no crowds. That's where I was today. It's unbelievable. This place is *unbelievable*.'

Dusk has moved in fast and the night air has a depth it doesn't have at home: the smell of timber, river, rain and roosters, of salt and smoke.

If only Matt would reach over, rest his fingers, lightly, on the inside of my thigh. Is that part of the deal? Can you do that when you're having a break from someone? I hadn't talked to Josh about parameters. We hadn't really talked about it at all.

It's as if Matt's read my mind. 'So what about your bloke? A break eh? That doesn't sound good.'

He leans toward me. 'If you guys are having a break, am I allowed to do this?' He brushes a strand of hair from my face, then lets his fingers linger for a moment on my cheek.

'I dunno. Maybe,' I murmur.

'Six months at Shane's is a tough gig, even for an extra five grand.' He lets his hand drop.

'I just don't feel like I can go back. It'd seem like I'd failed. And I'm bored at home. I mean Josh is telling me all the time that I should be using my head, aiming a bit higher than working at the backpackers, or the pub, says maybe I should enrol at uni.' I roll my head back. 'But I've just been feeling so trapped ... I had to get out. And maybe,' I hesitate. 'Well, maybe I'm not in love with him anymore.'

There. I said it.

'Then you've gotta tell him.'

'Tell him?' I repeat dumbly.

'You can't leave him hanging. That's not cool. That's not fair.'

'You're hardly one to talk!'

He shrugs with a half smile. 'Crack us another beer there?'

I do, fix one for myself, then tuck my knees under my chin.

It's between us now, this electric sense of possibility. Yes. No. Maybe. Maybe with more beer. I swerve, change subject. 'Anyway. I've been meaning to ask you. Abd al Hakim. You know him?'

'Abd al Hakim?' His accent is immaculate. He leans back. 'White beard, hooked nose, real tall? He's the head of Batu Batur's main mosque. Not the kind of bloke you want to piss off.'

'Shit.'

Matt arches a salt-stiff eyebrow and grins. 'Yeah?'

I tell him about the soccer game Abd al Hakim thought I started among the girls. 'I mean, I wish I'd stuck up for them. I totally think the girls here, whether they're in a jilbab or not, should have the opportunity to play sport if they want.'

Matt scrunches his brow in challenge. 'Yeah, but it's not really our place to change it. We don't live here. It's not our culture.'

Matt would feel this, profoundly, having grown up where he did, always on the outside.

'I agree with you, I guess, but I also think you can empower the women to start making the changes themselves. You can give them the tools, the ideas!'

'But that's just the point. The local crew here *don't want* Westerners coming in and telling them how to do things. Telling their women to tear off their jilbabs. Telling their men they can't fish from certain spots, 'cause now they're the private property of bules!'

His thumbnail snicks an agitated rhythm on the bottle. It's a long thumbnail, in the style of the ancient hero Bima, in the style of some of the men here.

'You talk about the empowerment of women. Have you heard of the women's sharia patrol up in Aceh?'

'I haven't.'

'Right. So there's this patrol unit up in Aceh. All chicks. They cruise around every Friday in the work ute and pick up blokes who've skipped the afternoon prayers. Fishermen havin' a quiet durry with their mates, fucken shop owners, you name it. The blokes get dragged back to the station and whipped.' He laughs cynically. 'Empowerment of women? I'd say the chicks have got all the empowerment they want.'

Matt slides down in his chair and places the bottle near his feet. 'Pen, just between you and me, I reckon Abd al Hakim is keen to get rid of all the expats here. It's partly due to Shane but there are also bigger issues at play. Think about the bombings.' He stabs his finger toward the earth, heavy with the smell of rain. 'This is your terrorist training ground right here. After East Java, the madrasah around Batu Batur are some of the most radical in the country.'

Madrasah. At home the word implies something rigid, dark, synonymous with terrorist training schools, evocative of bearded, backward men drilling the Qur'an into the heads of children, creating an army of Islamic automatons, of terrorists.

Matt lowers his voice. 'Listen, mate, I'm tellin' you this 'cause you're a pretty cool chick and I think you should be careful.'

I'm about to mention how it was probably Abd al Hakim here this morning, talking to Joni about something, when he stops the movement of my lips with a finger. Then he takes my hand. In a single, slow movement he pulls me from my chair and straddles me on his lap.

Slips my dress off my shoulders.

Brushes his nose, lightly, along my collarbone.

'Do you know what I've noticed about you, Penny?'

He bites the words into my throat with the white edges of his teeth.

'You ask a lot of questions, and you're a really good listener ...'

His cock strains toward me, against his boardies. I want him to nail me with it.

'... but you don't give much away about yourself.'

He takes my chin between his thumb and forefinger. I swoon, dizzy on his smell, dizzy with the feeling that I'm with a man who's strange, who's surging and fierce, who's looking at me like I'm earthy, a woman, not a doll, not a child, not a dream.

Suddenly a motorbike horn sounds over the fence and we both startle.

There's a man on the other side. Idling. Lighting up a kretek. He raises his hand. 'Hello Mister!' he calls.

27

In the morning I awake to find a single red hibiscus on the pillow next to me. My skin is singing. Last night was the first night in ages that I made love without thinking; without thoughts of the past, the future, without doubt. Matt was the circuit-breaker. I'm going to call Josh today. Break it. Tell him I'm staying for six months, maybe longer. Tell him it's over. If I can spend a night trembling under another man's touch, another man's tongue, and not feel even the slightest pang of remorse, then it should be over. Not that I expect anything more from Matt, because I don't, I don't dare.

I spend a little while moving around my room, sarong on hips, adjusting the sheets, smelling the pillows, rearranging my books of poetry. Then I grab my toiletries bag and a towel and bounce down the stairs toward the bathroom for a shower. There're only two: they're positioned side by side and separated by a wall – almost to the ceiling. I bang shut and lock the door, then unwind my sarong and hang it up on a hook.

In Indonesian bathrooms and toilets, there's usually a bak mandi: a big basin or a tub full of water. You scoop water from the bak mandi to flush the toilet or to wash. As I soap up, I find teeth-marks on the inside of my thighs. Feel a quick thrill. Mmm. I work shampoo through my hair then pour a saucepan-full of water over my head. With head tipped back, I notice something on the roof, a shard of something, a mirror.

What the hell is a mirror doing on the roof? I squeeze the soap from my hair, rinse my body, and move around, still looking up at the mirror but now from a different angle.

Reflected in that little bit of glass is a tiny, purple cock. It's being beaten back and forth, back and forth.

I want to scream. But I steel myself, tie my sarong above my boobs, race out and kick open the door of the bathroom next to me. The guy has his eyes closed. He doesn't notice me at first. I force a laugh. Point at his little dick and laugh. His eyes flutter open. And he flushes the same crimson-purple as his dick. Then he runs. Shoulders past me and runs. Down to the end of the garden and through the blue door and out onto the beach.

I feel like vomiting.

Ibu Ayu is nowhere to be seen and neither is Pak Joni. I rush up to my room, dress, then rush out; to town, to safety, where there're other people around.

My first stop is a shop on the main road selling mobile phones. I sort myself out with an Indonesian number and a SIM. No excuse now. Then I continue along the road to the supermarket, feeling a sluggish supply chain of sweat working its way from the roots of my hair to the inside of my thighs. Sometimes I bandage my thighs with cheap sarongs to stop them rubbing raw but I was too frantic this morning – hopefully the trousers will soak up most of the sweat and won't chafe. Every so often someone calls, 'Hello Mister!' and I force myself to look up and wave. Near the supermarket, something splits the skin above my ankle.

'What the …?!'

A group of kids in clag-coloured shorts are skittling rocks across the road at me.

I pick up the rock and throw it back. 'Little shits!'

They scatter with evil and lively grins.

The supermarket is artificially lit and polar-cooled. I move down the aisles, enjoying the air-conditioning, heart finally slowing. I'm craving chocolate. A little bottle of lemonade. I need some more soap. And I'm almost out of shampoo and conditioner. A man opens the door, letting in a thick oblong of smoky air. I linger in the air-conditioning until the shop assistant gives me a sideways look. As he scans my items, the slightest twitch of his nose divulges distaste. Three blocks of expensive chocolate? The *most* expensive shampoo and conditioner? I feel that guilt again, knowing I've just spent the equivalent of a week's wage on indulgences.

Back outside I'm greeted by an unmistakable squawk. The Kiwi. Marika leans sideways on her motorbike in a pair of tiny denim shorts. Her legs are gorgeous, crossed like elegant brown exclamation marks. Behind her yawns the dusky opening of a local grocery store with its begrimed aqua gallons and tails of laundry powder. I veer toward her. After my unsettling morning, I'm anxious for some company.

'Oh my god! Were you just shopping in the Circle K? You were, weren't you!' She smirks. 'You know, this is where all the locals shop.' She gestures behind her. 'It's half the price. And Ibu Nuri has the most adorable baby. A laki-laki. Oh – you do speak Bahasa don't you?'

'Cool, thanks for the heads-up,' I say, ignoring her question. She's a tough one to like, but after this morning, I'm not too keen on spending any more time alone. And given the outfit she's wearing, she must have some strategy to keep the stalkers at bay. 'Are you busy at the moment? Do you wanna go for a coffee or something?'

She wraps a set of manicured fingers around the motorbike handle. 'Actually, I'm off to work.'

'Oh yeah. Where do you work?'

'I've got a business here.'

'What's your business?'

'IT.'

'IT?'

'Yeah. I've started an internet cafe. First one in Batu Batur.'

'An internet cafe? I didn't think there was any internet! Where is it? Do you reckon I could grab a lift?'

She seems stumped by my enthusiasm.

'Well, if you like. I haven't managed to get a place right in the centre of town. It's just on the outskirts. Near Dennis and Meri's.'

'No worries, I can walk back into town.'

'Fine.'

She keeps the bike steady with those killer legs and guns it to life.

We head through town, skewing wildly around puddles and oxen and men pedalling becaks. Marika's bare legs don't go unnoticed. Some of the older men gape and grin. Others are less impressed; their faces contract in indignation and spite. The younger people are the most shocked. One young woman sends a pellet of spit after us. A young man throws a stick.

By the time we get to the internet cafe, I wish I hadn't been seen with her. You have to be respectful with what you wear. Especially here. It's not Kuta or the Gilis. But who am I to be on a soapbox about dress codes?

I expected quirkiness in the Kiwi's cafe, or a Balinese élan – incense and air-con. Instead, there are the typical plastic booths with at least three people crowded around each computer and a stale grey smell of kretek smoke. The floor is textured with ash and plastic wrappers.

She swans in and an employee at the master computer straightens his back, mouse moving frantically. Then his features relax. Marika doesn't appear to notice.

'Joko.' Her tone is professional, even disdainful. 'Dua kopi hitam, ya. Cepat!'

Joko jumps up.

'You drink Indo coffee?'

'Of course.'

She leads me to her office out the back.

The office is immaculate, individualised only by a potted aloe plant and a few photos. Marika cheek-to-cheek with a handsome bloke; Marika pulling into a stormy, serious barrel, wetsuited and game-faced; Marika with her arm around a woman who shares her sharp nose.

'Is that your mum?'

She looks at the photo. 'Yeah. She lives on the North Island, in Mahia.'

'Do you miss her?'

'A bit.'

Marika wouldn't be older than twenty-four. Probably a year or two older than me. What a gutsy venture, heading out to a remote town in Sumatra, setting up a business, learning Indo, surfing solo. Working for someone else in a bule-only surf camp seems tame in comparison.

'Have you been here for long?'

'Not really. Not as long as Matt. He's been coming for about five years. Has a lot of really close local friends. I've only been here nine months but I started this place two months ago.'

'Do you like Batu Batur?'

She slides her thong back and forth across the ground. I've never seen a high-heeled thong before.

'When I first got here, I loved it. Now, it's okay.'

There it is again, that challenge, but softer now, as if she's trying to convince herself as much as me.

'I felt welcome when I first moved here. The people seemed mellow, nearly everyone was friendly. My neighbours,' she gestures to either side, 'were always dropping in with leftover rice, tempe, chicken. They still do, they're legends. I let 'em use the internet for free.'

She stops sliding her foot and starts seesawing a pen between her fingers. 'In the last two months though, the vibe has changed. I mean maybe there was always some hostility. Because of Shane. But I dunno. I feel as if it's more than that now.'

'Yeah, I have to admit, I haven't exactly felt safe here over the last week.'

'After Franz's?'

'Well, sure. But I was thinking more the blokes.'

'Ah.' She lifts her eyebrows. They're expertly waxed.

Something shifts, there's a softening. We're warming to each other. Fraternising. The way women do when there are no blokes around.

So I tell her about this morning in the shower. It must happen all the time – at home as well as here – but I still feel rattled. Dirty in my skin.

She tilts her head to the side. 'I've had guys wait for me a couple of times on the sand when I've been out surfing by myself. Most of the time they're harmless. As soon as you speak a bit of Indo or better still, Lampung, it trashes whatever myths they have from whatever porn films they've watched. They realise you're an actual person. You remind them by telling them they've got sisters and mothers. Most times they'll ask you to come home and have dinner with their family!'

'Yeah, I thought it was a bit like that.' The office feels like the inside of a rice-cooker and I hope there's not a sweat patch on the bum of my trousers.

The Kiwi isn't perturbed. She looks cool and classy in her

denim shorts and Parisian thongs. She chucks the pen at the wall.

'Anyway, I got a few bits and pieces I gotta do around here. You coming over to Dennis' in a couple of nights?'

'I dunno. Yeah. Maybe. What's happening?'

'Just a barbecue. A bit of a chat about how we can cut a lower profile. And Matt's gunna fill us in on where we're at with Shane.'

'Shane? What's Matt got to do with Shane?'

'Matt hasn't said anything to you?'

I shake my head.

'Maybe he's worried you'll warn Shane. Oh well. Come to Dennis' and you'll find out.'

What the hell? I sit for a moment in uncomfortable indecision – should I press her for details? I let it slide. 'Can you tell me where you got your eyebrows waxed and your nails done? I got the worst wax the other day and my nails ...'

The Kiwi promptly draws me a map. 'The lady who runs it is from Surabaya – she's an absolute character! But she's closed Fridays and Sundays. Now, did you say you wanted to use the net?'

Marika gets up briskly and I follow her back out into the smoky cafe. All the computers are full. She looks around. Then walks over to two young guys in school uniforms. They're glued to a game. Guns, blood, khaki-coloured animation.

'Get off,' she tells them in Indo.

I try to protest but she waves her fingertips at me.

'Don't worry about it. It's not like they're doing anything important.'

The boys shuffle sullenly toward the door.

28

Three hours later I step outside with the strain of a headache behind my eyes. It's from the glare of the screen, the tidal movement of cigarette smoke between the booths, the multiple cups of black coffee. I picked up an email from Dad and another from my sister Lucy, the kind of travel email that's sent in bulk. She's the brains of the family, a law graduate with distinction who's spent the last year drinking tequila with dark-eyed villains and drug runners in Mexico. We've both definitely got more of Dad in us than Mum, more wildness than caution.

Nothing from Mum, but that's not unusual. As a kid I remember her constant worry, constant disapproval. As an adult, I recognise a natural pessimist. When I decided to go to Bali with Dad, Mum was beside herself. It's probably only now I've begun to acknowledge how much I hurt her. She met Dad in Indo in the late '70s and they fell in love. But it's as if her memory of this country has been soured; she hasn't been back since they split up when I was twelve. Now she's living over East, doing the rich hippy thing at Byron Bay, a moderately successful interior designer.

Nothing from Josh either. Instead, I clicked through photos on the company website of a 'team-building' night they had recently in the city. Josh looked like he was ten schooners deep, flashing those fine, dark, private-school-boy eyes at the women around him, the first grey threads through his dark hair.

Back at the bungalows I'll charge up my phone, send him a message, arrange a time to talk.

I wave down a becak. The seat probably fits four Indonesian bums to my one. The man is perched on the bicycle behind me. He kicks off the curb. 'Ibu Ayu's bungalows,' I tell him. We creak along the left-hand side of the road, skirting puddles and goats with jangling brass necklaces. I keep looking at the sky, expecting it'll start raining. The becak rider doesn't look to the sky, or to the sea, or to the pensive, gloom-fringed mountains. He stares straight ahead, expression bleached of dream or whim. Only his legs move, with effort. When we finally arrive at the bungalows I give him an extra twenty thousand rupiah. For a moment, there's a greedy gleam in his pupils. Then it dims, as if he's already spent the money, as if his wife has already demanded he hand it over. He turns a slow, speechless semicircle and pedals back to town.

Ibu Ayu is on the dining deck peeling a snake fruit. The skin of the fruit lies in puzzle pieces between her forearms. 'Penny!' she calls out. 'Kenapa kamu nggak mau sarapan?' Why didn't you want breakfast?

I join Ibu on the deck and accept a piece. The salak is dry and tart, a little like an apple, a little like an unripe pear. While I'm crunching, I explain what happened in the shower. She's horrified.

'Maaf sekali Penny, aduh! Where's Joni?'

'Don't – no, don't call Bapak! It's okay. There's no-one around now.'

I resist an urge to look over the guesthouse wall to the tree line.

'It's not your fault. Penny always dress, ahh, how you say?'

'Sensibly?'

'Exactly. In long shirt, long skirt, like Indonesian lady, ya? But the problem is, sometimes the girl coming here, for example, I had girls six month ago from France. French girl Rip Curl team, you know? All surfing, making film.'

A look between consternation and wonder settles on her face.

'These girls go away surfing in the morning, then in the afternoon they come back and surfing again, just here, out front.' She waves a contemptuous hand toward the water. 'But then – and this is the problem – after they surfing, they sunbake! In bikini! Just here on the beach! Wah!'

She pushes the salak peels into a spiky square.

'So I say, "Now listen you girl. No sunbaking here. No good. All these men watching you!" And you know what those girl say to me? They stick their chest out like this and they say: "So what? Let them look!"'

I laugh at Ibu's animation.

A hot spool of thunder unravels.

'But that's not all. Now I have friends at the market who won't take their children to the beach to swim. They don't want them to see lady in bikini.'

While I'm thinking of how to answer her, a door swings open on the main building, Cahyati's foot eases a bag into the doorway. Cahyati's getting the sack. Maybe it's because she took me to the soccer game.

'Ada apa, Bu? Cahyati ke mana?'

'Cahyati mau pulang kampung. Just for one, maybe two night.'

I swallow with relief. 'Why's she heading home?'

'Her mother sick.'

'Sakit?' Sick?

'Always sakit,' she mutters. 'Cahyati finish school at fourteen, so she could look after her mother. She was very smart and

Joni and I help pay for a good madrasah, best madrasah in the area! Then mother sick – finish.'

Matt said the madrasah around Batu Batur were some of the most radical in the country.

'Why did you send her to a madrasah, not a normal SMP or SMA?'

'Ya, if you want focus on Islamic education, you send your children to madrasah. Or better still, to pesantren, like an Islamic boarding school. Madrasah, pesantren, all over Indonesia. Some tourist tell me in Australia you have Christian school, no? Same here. We have Islamic school.'

Cahyati steps from the main door of the building and picks up her bag. I think we have the idea at the same time but Ibu speaks first. 'How about you go with her? When you start work at Shane's you won't get time to visit the mountains. Cahyati's village is very traditional, very beautiful.'

An excitement, a lightening of my heart is swiftly undercut by the thought I'd rather stay here in case Matt comes by. Then I curse myself for being so ungracious. If Cahyati is happy to take me to her village for a night or two, then I'm happy to go.

'Cahyati!' bawls Ibu.

Cahyati makes her way to the dining deck. The two women converse quickly in Bahasa Lampung and I can see from her eager nods she's keen to have me.

'Okay,' Ibu turns away from Cahyati. 'She say she leave on the four o'clock bus from the market. You get some things now and you go together. Bapak Joni take you to the market on the motorbike.'

I run back to my bungalow to grab my toothbrush and a couple of changes of undies.

29

Two hours later we're hurtling knees-to-chin toward the mountains. I nurse a basket of dried sardines for an old, half-blind man and Cahyati's thongs rest on a chook's cage. When Cahyati starts to doze, I reach into my bag for my water bottle. It's filled with gin. After the incident that morning and mindful of the bus trip ahead, I'm craving a few hours of drunken dreamy indifference. I'm careful not to drink too much. If anyone notices, I'll probably be hauled off the bus and stoned. And I don't want to end up busting for a wee. We might go for hours and hours without a stop.

I turn my face toward the fading afternoon. There's the usual smell of burning rubbish and a hint of something else, sweet as cedar and aromatic as sandalwood. The first lamps bloom orange in the rice fields and kaki lima smoke by the roadside. Across the aisle the old man whose sardines I'm nursing beams and winks his one good eye. He points at my water bottle and winks again. I pass the bottle over. He takes a swig, smacks his lips in delight, then hands it back. I ask him something in Indonesian. He answers in Lampung. We laugh, realising we have no common language, content to trade sips and grins.

Just as we begin the climb into the mountains, there are two young women walking along the side of the road. They balance woven baskets on their heads and wear sarongs that brush their ankles. They walk with a grace rare in young women at home – nothing like the drunken, high-heeled hobble of beautiful girls in Perth. Upon seeing the girls, the bus driver and conductor let out hisses of approval. Then, instead of showing their appreciation through horn or shout, the driver wrenches the steering wheel and veers toward them. The girl closest to the road trips in fright and spills her basket of custard apples. The other keeps her balance and shakes her fist at the bus. Both the driver and conductor dissolve into childish giggles.

Disgusted, I pull my eyes from the road and dig out my phone. What should I write to Josh? 'Hey Josh, here's my new number …', 'Hey Josh, everything's going well …' Then I hold the phone and just sit, remembering the first night we met. I was living in a share house in Freo, hot off a four-month trip bartending on Namotu in Fiji. One of Dad's mates has shares in the resort and he'd lined me up with a job. I had a good suntan and was fit from two surfs a day, but after four months on a tiny island, I was ready for a change. I planned to come back to WA, spend six months working, then fly over to Indo for the next drift. I snapped up a job at a bar in Freo and two weeks after I started, Josh walked through the door. I noticed him straight away. His dark hair cut to the jaw. The width of his shoulders. When one of the other girls moved to serve him I nudged her out of the way.

'What can I get you tonight?'

'A Coopers.'

He took his beer to a corner. He was alone. All night, his eyes tracked me. At last, with the candles running low on their wicks, we started talking. Not only was he handsome, but he was really smart, and really sad. He'd just separated from his wife. A week later we met for coffee. Eight months later, I'd quit my job at the bar in Freo, moved out of the share house to Scarborough, and we'd booked a two-week holiday to Bali together. I thought I was in love.

I look back down at my phone, punch in, 'Hey Josh, would love to chat soon. Msg me a time that suits.' I hit 'send'. Less than a minute later, the signal drops out completely.

The road steepens and we slow. Dusk crushes into the valleys, catches under the leaves. I'm grateful – the memory of the head-on on the way to Batu Batur is still vivid, and on trips like this, it's better not to look, better to travel in the dark. We pass the turn-off to Franz and Adalie's and from there the road is unfamiliar. I must drift off because the next thing I remember is Cahyati shaking me awake saying, 'Sudah nyampai.'

We're let off at the edge of the road. Columns of black jungle press in on either side and there's the manic shrieking of insects. 'We walk now,' she says to me. 'It's about half an hour.'

'Okay, yuk!' Let's go!

A breeze shifts the canopy, shivers down cupfuls of cold rain.

30

Cahyati's mum doesn't look sick; she nurses one child and dandles another on her knee while offering an endless stream of observation and anecdote. Every now and then she slaps at the running legs of the two other children, telling them to settle down, that it's time for bed.

'Nakal!' she says with feeling.

Her house is simple but spotless; the wooden floor has been swept clean and there are no roaches or rats nibbling at the edge of the light.

One of Cahyati's little sisters brings us bowls of watery jack-fruit curry. Then she slips clear of her mum's hand and races outside. She must have told her friends there's a bule staying at her house because as we eat, tiny foreheads lift above the windowsills and fingers curl around the doorframe. By the end of the night half the village has gathered around the house.

Cahyati makes me a bed on a cane mat in the room she shares with her sisters. She gives me a hairy blanket but as soon as it rests on my skin I start to itch. Bedbugs, for sure. If I throw the blanket out the window it'll probably lift up and scuttle away. I push it aside, grateful, nonetheless, for how accommodating Cahyati's family has been. Sometimes in people's homes and villages, you get sly suggestions to take husbands or children back to Australia; addresses copied carefully into the back of guidebooks and diaries, each letter shaped with the fiercest hope. Cahyati's mum didn't mention a thing – even the presence of a bule didn't seem to perturb her; she just looked happy to see her eldest daughter. Cahyati's dad, who came in later, smiled at me, then went and quietly smoked a kretek by the open door.

31

Cahyati and I wash in the river. There's a pool for women and, upriver, a pool for men. The women's pool is dammed with valley rocks and enclosed by lianas and ferns. I copy Cahyati, keeping a sarong tied above my boobs and washing my body inch by inch from my wrists to the cracks between my toes. No tinea yet.

Despite the cold, I scrub my skin raw with a nailbrush. My Indonesian friends are fastidious about washing. 'Sudah mandi?' I'm often asked. Have you had a wash? It's such a personal question; you'd never ask anyone this at home! Even though no harm is meant it always makes me prickly and indignant. What do you reckon? Of course I have!

'Mandi lagi!' they tell me, shaking fingers. Wash again!

By the time we've washed, done the laundry and helped Cahyati's mum prepare lunch and dinner, it's past midday. The dead hours close around us and we relocate to the balcony. There's no wind to displace the humidity; it's trapped under the clouds, trapped between the wooden walls of the homes.

Cahyati is completely different here at home with her nan and her mum and her siblings. There's a lightness about her. If you passed her on the street in Batu Batur, you probably wouldn't think she was a knockout. But here, with her teeth flashing, skin glossy and her jilbab slung over the back of a chair – she has a gorgeous, almost Papuan afro of hair – you'd definitely look twice. How dependent beauty can be on one's mood. I think some women are at their most beautiful when pensive or sulking. Not so for Cahyati. I'd cast her as a victim, as someone to be pitied, stooped under the weight of Ibu Ayu's derision, when in fact she is strong and glowing and beautiful in her own space, in her own way.

How awful we women can be to each other.

I sit with my back against the wall, legs stretched out. Cahyati is sprawled on her belly. It's too hot to move. Across the road, there's a tiny shop. It sells things like instant coffee and kerupuks. Two women sit side by side in rattan chairs. The older woman is a nenek, a grandmother, probably in her late sixties. She has three teeth in a face that's both sweet and spicy – no shadows of melancholy or malice are cast in her wrinkles. The nenek cackles and chain-smokes and insults her customers, always smiling. The other woman looks to be her daughter, or daughter-in-law. She's probably in her late thirties and also has a kind of cheeky defiance in her gesture and appearance that seems to run counter to culture and religion. She's a handsome woman with hair to her waist, lipsticked lips and a sleeveless dress. The two women share a cigarette. It doesn't smell of the soft blaze of cloves, but is cigar-like, wrapped in dark brown paper. I wonder why neither of them covers their hair and why the younger woman has bare arms.

After a while, when the trickle of customers has stopped, the nenek stretches herself out on the floorboards and starts snoring. I don't know any elderly people at home who could do that! Here, the old people aren't shut away. They continue to be part of the community, they sit out the front of the shops, sweep leaves, collect wood, play with grandkids; in Batu Batur, old men ride straight-backed on classical bicycles, gripping bamboo fishing rods. Even the older people with Alzheimer's still have a place and are looked out for by the rest of the community. Everyone has a place.

32

The next morning, the nenek is sitting out the front looking very prim and demure in a headscarf. I can't help myself. 'Hey Nenek,' I call out in Indonesian. 'How come you're wearing a headscarf this morning?' The nenek's three teeth glisten in a grin. 'Dingin!' she shouts back. It's cold!

We're running late for the bus. Cahyati's mum showered us with treats for the road and then invented a number of reasons to delay our departure: could Cahyati help her little sister get dressed? Could I pull up a couple of buckets of water from the well so Ibu could do the laundry? Could Cahyati duck over to one of the neighbour's houses to humbug some eggs?

At last we're off. We climb over tree roots and step around hair-heavy ropes of vine. Every now and then we catch the curl of a monkey's tail, the swift snap of a bat's wings. After a while the vegetation opens up. We didn't come this way the other day.

I turn to Cahyati but before I can ask anything she grips my hand and whispers, 'It's a shortcut.'

We're standing in front of a clearing. It isn't unusual in any physical way, just an oblong of dark earth the size of a small soccer field. But there's something eerie about it. The trees around the edge, rather than reaching toward the light as they should, seem to lean back against each other, to huddle away from the space.

I've heard about places like this. Places that get under your skin. Old places.

It comes down fast. I feel physically sick. The sick of unborn babies, prawns turned toxic, underwater hold-downs.

'Lewat sini?' I ask nervously.

'Iya, this way. Ready?'

She wrenches my hand and we take off at a sprint. I run as if all the stalkers in Batu Batur are after me. I run with a feeling in my gut like a fishing knife is curving in and out. I run faster than I ever have at basketball, or athletics, or when I used to sprint to the surf in the morning before school.

It's wrong. The place is wrong. And with every footstep I know we shouldn't be here.

We get to the other side but Cahyati doesn't slow, keeps running, until finally we see the road.

And then Cahyati is bailing me up, saying low and urgent, 'Don't tell my mum, don't tell Ibu Ayu, don't tell anyone we went that way, okay?'

Moments later, the bus swings into view, seedy Indonesian dangdut pumping from its speakers.

33

Dusk falls wet along the guesthouse paths, along the pitching roofs. Matt's waiting on the balcony of my bungalow, his head back, his eyes closed.

'Hey Matt, what's goin' on?'

His head jolts forward.

He looks like he hasn't slept. He obviously hasn't been surfing. There's no shadow of zinc across the bridge of his nose, no scrawls of wind or salt or sun.

'Are you okay?'

'You got beer?'

'I'm all out. Do you want me to go down and check with Ibu Ayu?'

'Nah. How about gin?'

There's a drizzle left in my water bottle. 'Not enough for a shot.'

'Alright.' He slaps the tops of his legs. 'Put that inside and let's go. You keen for a feed? There's a warung in town where we can have a drink and get a decent nasi campur.'

'A drink? Like, a real drink?'

'Yeah.'

'Okay, let's do it.' As I slip past him, I wonder if he'll own it, what happened the other night. He surprises me. Catches my fingers and kisses them. Gracious. Succinct. I chuck my stuff inside, allow myself a secret smile and turn the key.

34

The warung is tucked away from the main street and lit with one of those harsh, off-white electric lights that exposes every blemish. The place is packed with blokes tucking in to nasi campur with their fingers and sipping from plastic cups.

'Arak,' Matt says as we nudge our way to a spare table in the corner.

Some of the men stop eating and stare at us, others greet us with slurry 'Hello Misters!' and a few seem to know Matt, because they wink and leer as we squeeze into our seats.

'Arak, did you say? Rice wine? In the cups?'

Matt nods.

'How do they get away with it?'

'It's run by an Indo-Chinese family. They've been here generations. I asked Pak Wu about it and he says he pays a monthly bribe to the police so they'll turn a blind eye. Here he is.'

Pak Wu comes out of the kitchen with an enamel jug and a sneering razor of a mouth. He reminds me of the cook in a Somerset Maugham short story. The cook lifts his eyebrows and the jug.

'Definitely,' Matt says, 'and two nasi campur.'

The cook places the jug on the table next to us and waddles back to the kitchen.

'So you weren't round last night?' Matt catches my hand and plays his thumb against my thumb.

'Nah.'

'Where were ya? I thought you must have pissed off. That's what Ibu Ayu said.'

What a schemer!

'So how'd ya know I'd be back tonight?'

'Well, Ibu didn't exactly look her honest self.'

'Ha.'

'So where were ya?' It comes across hot with query and ownership.

I look carefully at his face. What do I really know about him? Not much. I like his smell. And the way he fucks, creative and savage and intense. He's a pilot, though he doesn't quite fit the ironed-at-the-edges look you'd expect. And he too has a connection, an affinity to this place, that runs much deeper than your average surf tourist. I know that I want to know more.

'So?' he prompts again.

'I went to Cahyati's place up in the mountains.'

'Oh yeah. Beautiful country up there.'

'It sure was, but there was this ...'

'There was what?'

I'm not sure whether to tell him about our mad dash across the clearing. Maybe he's too rational, not intuitive enough to understand. Then I remember what he said about a flight path to Nias being cancelled because the Javanese he was working with were worried about black magic. There had been no disbelief in his tone.

So I tell him about crossing the clearing, ask if he knows the place, if he's ever been to a place like this.

'I don't know the spot you're talking about. But the local people probably believe there are spirits there. It could be sacred, it could be an old grave site. I think there are some places where the earth holds a memory, and the energy there can be really dark or really strong. Like, have you ever been to the Tuol Sleng Museum in Cambo?'

I shake my head.

'I knew nothing about the prison when I visited. It was a clear day. Hot, no clouds. As soon as I stepped inside I got head-to-toe goosebumps. I had about half an hour in there, wandering along the corridors, and then I started to feel really nauseous. I thought I was going to throw up. So I ran outside and the feeling disappeared.'

Matt takes a sip of arak and continues. 'I gave myself five minutes, and then went back in. The nausea hit me again. I felt like I was seconds away from throwing up. So I rushed back out. And it went away. It was the strangest thing, the energy was so crook. My brain could rationalise it but my spirit ... There's heaps of places like this. Hampi, in India, is really creepy. Port Arthur, in Tassy – now *that* place is fucked.'

The cook interrupts with bowls of water. Matt dips in his right hand, says, 'When I was a kid growing up in Vanuatu, there was this cave about ten kilometres out of the village. No-one ever went near it. They said a woman-spirit lived in the cave and that if she saw you, and looked in your eyes, you'd go mad. I went out there a couple of times with some of my friends on our pushies. You could ride about halfway before the track through the jungle became too bad. The first time we went, two of us got flat tyres. The second time we went, I came down with typhoid a day later. The third time, just as we neared the cave, one of my mates slipped and broke his leg. It was an absolute mission getting him back to the village.'

The cook slides plates of nasi campur in front of us. It looks good. Oily purple cubes of eggplant, red chilli sambal, water spinach, tempe and a few chunks of earthy rendang border a perfect tower of rice. But it takes me a moment to regain my appetite.

'You didn't go back a fourth time?'

'No way.'

'So what do you reckon about this clearing near Cahyati's?'

'Your guess is as good as mine. I tell you who might know though: Franz. He's got some interesting perspectives on the way the local crew here mix up their traditional beliefs and Islam. We'll probably catch him tonight.'

I rinse my hand in the plastic bowl then gather a ball of rice and sambal between my fingers. 'What's happening tonight?'

'Dennis and Meri are having a barbecue. Told 'em we'd swing past after dinner for a drink.'

The barbecue the Kiwi had been on about. Something about Matt filling everyone in on 'where we're at with Shane'. I pick at my campur. Those stories give me a sense that there's a depth to him, a perceptiveness. But I also can't help feeling there's something else, something secretive and not quite truthful – what does that mean: 'where we're at with Shane'?

'Ibu Ayu said you had a bit of a scare,' Matt says.

'A scare?'

Of course. I haven't seen him since he stayed over. And the next morning there was that bloke in the shower. So I tell him what happened and for about half a second he looks horrified and then he starts to laugh. He laughs and laughs and says, 'Penny, I can't say that I blame him!'

Maybe, if it were six months down the track, if I had ten grand saved up, a toffee-coloured tan, a ticket onward, I'd be laughing with him. But just now, in this warung where the air is thick and bright as white fungus, and where a bunch of blokes are leering and guzzling arak and beer, I can't join him.

'Sorry, Pen,' he says. 'This used to happen to my missus all the time. She was pretty, like you, but taller, and dark. Won Kimberley Girl when she was nineteen. She was a major princess, a major headcase. But I guess it's different for you.'

'Oh?'

He takes my hand. I don't return his squeeze.

'You're a lot more independent. You're a lot more reserved. I get the impression that you're alright, you know, that you can look after yourself.'

I don't answer.

The Chinese cook comes up to our table and refills our cups. I recoil slightly from his bitter garlicky breath, pull my hand from Matt's.

'WC di mana, Pak?' Where's the loo?

He ignores me, tells Matt.

As I stand, Matt reaches out, plants a kiss like a sticker on my wrist. Frustrating, how sometimes men can't admit when they've hurt you. But promising, how he talked about his missus in the past tense.

I push out through the plastic flaps at the back of the warung into a filthy oil-coloured room. The toilet is through another door to the left. I gag in horror. I've been in a lot of scary toilets (the ones on ferries are usually revolting) but this is by far the worst. It's a typical Indo squat toilet, with a saucepan-like bucket to wash your bum and a bak mandi. The toilet is unflushed: diarrhoea has made a yellow lake-line around the bowl, but worse than this is that the toilet also doubles as a kitchen. Forks and spoons half-float in wet piles, a teetering stack of bowls lean against a wall and a few grubby plates float in the bak mandi itself.

I nearly turn around and walk out, but I'm busting.

In the fifty-five seconds it takes me to wee and get back, Matt's been shanghaied into a game of chess. Tables have been rearranged, chairs pulled close. The men are putting bets on who they think will win. Matt looks up and sees me at the edge of the crowd – he gestures for me to push through to the seat saved next to him. When I sit he draws his thumbnail along my thigh. A subtle, but firm sign of ownership. For the next three quarters of an hour it's as if I'm invisible.

'What about Dennis'? Won't we be late?' I ask between moves.

'Probably.' Matt kisses my neck and goes back to the game.

35

When we finally get to Dennis', the courtyard is full of motorbikes. Behind us, along the street, gaunt, cunning dogs wet their teeth in each other's throats. At the door, Matt lets go of my hand.

'Oh finally, Matthew!' The Kiwi stands up and greets him with a kiss on the cheek. She greets me next with an insincere embrace, still talking over her shoulder to Matt. When she steps back she looks different to the day before. Tiny denim shorts have been replaced with sailor-loose, beige pants. She's changed up a boob-exposing singlet with a baggy t-shirt. She still looks fantastic.

I step forward and introduce myself to a Chinese woman, who I learn is the cook's wife, to an old Pommy bloke with a white moustache, and to Rick, a young developer from WA. Rick's handsome, solid, he got rich quick in the mines in the Pilbara and is now building a string of luxury villas between Batu Batur and Shane's. Franz and his wife Adalie acknowledge me; Dennis grins and Meri waves from the kitchen.

After the initial introductions we hear the latest.

'Go on, Rick, you better tell them,' says the Kiwi, flicking her hair.

He tells us that when he checked the worksite that morning, his staff were dragging on kreteks and blinking lazily at piles of rubble where, yesterday, three almost-completed villas had stood.

'No-one bothered to call the boss, did they? No-one bothered to call me!'

'What happened to your security guard?' Matt asks.

Rick scowls. 'What d'you reckon, mate? He disappeared, of course. Hasn't been seen since last night –'

'Tell them, Rick, tell them what they did,' urges Marika.

'Get this,' he addresses Matt, 'looks like they used a truck.'

'A truck?' Matt drawls.

'Yeah, that's what I said. They certainly didn't use a fucken becak. They backed into three of the villas, just rammed them until –'

'Unbelievable,' Matt interrupts.

Rick's lip lifts in a snarl.

'I'm so sorry to hear that, mate,' Matt adds, flawlessly sincere.

With effort, Rick reassembles his mouth. Some women might find that mouth sensuous.

'So,' Matt continues, 'broken windows one week, then crew bulldozing businesses the next. What are you guys thinking? Are you packing it in or gunna stick it out?'

Pearly coils of citronella unspin and circle our ankles.

'Well, we're going back to Europe,' says Franz. 'In thirty-five years of living in Indonesia, all through Indonesia, we have never felt so …' he hesitates, reaches for the right word, settles with, 'uncomfortable. We will go back to Europe. And then maybe some day we try Flores.'

His grey-haired wife puts a hand on his knee.

The couple have an obvious passion for the culture, for the country. Their home is testament to that, as, no doubt, is Franz's anthropological work. Do they feel betrayed by the people, by this place? And if such a grounded and empathetic couple could be targeted, then what might be in store for someone like Shane?

Dennis' wife says softly, 'Maybe it's time for some dessert, ya?'

Murmurs of agreement.

'And the rest of you?'

'Well I'm gunna see these villas go up,' Rick says. 'Should be able to get back what I've lost on insurance. Whatever's going on now will settle down. In ten years they'll be worth shitloads. Got plans to run exclusive surf tours to outer reefs even Matt doesn't know about.'

Matt ignores him.

I half-listen to the answers of the rest of the group, half-listen to Meri in the kitchen. There's the banging of spoons and cupboards, the suck of the fridge sealing shut. What does she think about all this – about Dennis' guests and their 'us and them' mentality, criticisms of the people, her people? By the time she brings out bowls of sticky rice drizzled with condensed milk, everyone else has said they're staying put.

'Next, then,' says Matt. 'If we're staying, we've gotta deal with Shane.'

'Dealing with Shane won't solve anything,' says Dennis quietly.

I like Dennis. He has the slow calm of a man with the tropics in his blood.

'The Indonesians are not always that welcoming to outsiders, full stop. Only a few years ago, Indo-Chinese were being raped, persecuted, burned alive. Now, in this instance, just getting rid of one man –'

'Yeah, but,' Rick interrupts bullishly. 'The difference is, we're spending money. The Indos are getting our money. Even Shane is doing his bit to boost the economy. The Chinese hoarded it and kept it to themselves. We hand out. Just look at Bali, mate.'

Dennis pushes his glasses up the bridge of his nose and continues patiently. 'You may be right that money from tourism will solve it, down the track. But at the moment, we simply don't have the luxury of time to wait for the locals to appreciate these flow-on effects. From what I gather, from what Meri has heard in the community, it was a couple of radical young men who threw the rocks at Franz and Adalie's – and I use the word "radical" carefully. But they are known to be affiliated with a militant Islamist group with wider reach. Now whether that's Darul Islam or Jemaah Islamiyah or someone else, we don't know. But, Meri's suggestion,' – Meri steps from the kitchen and rests her weight against the doorframe, tea towel in hand – 'is that it would be best to approach Abd al Hakim directly and give a sizeable donation to the mosque. He is in more of a position to control and influence young men like this, because he has the ear of the whole community, can mobilise the community against them. At the moment, he has no motivation to do this. But for the right price ...'

Rick says under his breath, 'That towel-headed bastard won't get a cent from me.'

There's the trace of a smile on the cook's wife's lips.

Rick says louder, with muscle, 'So who was it then that bulldozed my villas? Are you saying it was these radical cunts?'

'I'm saying we negotiate with Hakim so that we all stay safe.'

No-one answers. Matt leans back. Manages to command the attention of the group with this single movement.

'I think Dennis is right,' he says. 'I think that's a good way to go about it. But I've also been working with Bapak Joni on a different strategy. We've been to see a dukun.'

'A dukun?' pipes up the English bloke for the first time. 'A fucking dukun? Are you serious, man?'

The Kiwi looks smug. That's obviously what she was referring to at the internet cafe.

Dennis puts his head in his hands.

'To make Shane sick,' Matt says. 'Less trouble. Just for a while, just while things settle down.'

The night I met Shane he'd winced and buckled and grabbed his gut. Is he sick? I asked the girl. No, not sick. I remember Matt and Joni talking that morning, and Matt asking me, after we'd had a surf together, how Shane had seemed. It doesn't surprise me, Matt going to the local black magician. From what I've heard, there's still plenty of black magic in the Solomon Islands and Vanuatu. Matt would have grown up around it.

'Bullshit.' Rick sneers. 'It's a load of bullshit.' He turns to me, even though I've been watchfully silent. 'Your hippy mate here might think there's such a thing –'

Matt springs to his feet. Rick tenses. We all tense.

But Matt ignores him and starts collecting the empty bowls. Meri rushes forward to help but he waves her away. I follow him to the kitchen. He fills Meri's sink. I add a squirt of green detergent then hand him the bowls, one after the other. They make a percussive sound as Matt stacks them, clean, on the other side.

'When do you go back to work?' I ask without looking at him.

'Coupla days,' he says.

'Before you go, will you take me to the dukun?' My voice trembles. As a kid I always had the feeling that the uneasy line between the spiritual and the physical was easier to cross here than at home. This chance, to go and visit a dukun … it is rarely something you can even talk about with local people, let alone experience firsthand.

'No.'

I take his hand. 'Please?'

He says nothing and we're saved from silence by the sound of a text message. I pull out my phone, wondering if Josh has replied. Then I realise Matt has the same message tone, and it's not for me. A bright strand of hair is caught in his stubble and it takes all my willpower to resist reaching over and drawing it free. He puts his phone away.

'Sorry, Pen, I won't be able to give you a lift home. I'm sure

Dennis will take you after everyone's left. I'll see you tomorrow. We should go up to the hot springs. When do you start at Shane's?'

It takes me a beat to answer. What's so important that Matt has to race off without giving me a lift?

'In a coupla days,' I say.

'Righto.'

The Kiwi's voice bounces after him into the courtyard: 'But Matthew ...!'

And then he's gone.

I go back to my chair, to the now-struggling conversation. It's obvious the group doesn't get together often. The only thing they really have in common is that they're all outsiders.

Before she leaves, Adalie asks for my number. 'We're starting to pack soon. I will send a message in case there is anything you might like. We won't be able to take everything.'

I thank her warmly and soon I'm the only one left, waiting in the kitchen while geckos zigzag the walls.

'That Matt's a scoundrel,' Dennis says after he and Meri have seen off Rick and the Kiwi, 'leaving you here to walk home. I'll give you a lift after a cup of tea.'

'Oh, I don't want to be any trouble. I'm more than happy to walk. It's not that far.'

'Don't be ridiculous!'

He heads into the kitchen and I help Meri carry the extra chairs back out onto the front balcony. Her lips and nails are a loud proud red and she's pencilled on a beauty spot just to the left of her lower lip. Her hair is cropped short and uncovered.

'Have you been to Australia?'

'Of course. Nice for holiday but if you stay there for too long: pusing,' she taps her head. 'And, sorry ya, but also a little bit boring!'

'Boring?!'

We laugh.

Years ago, I met a young Balinese guy who fell in love with an Australian girl, got her pregnant and found himself bailed up in Bunbury with a bub and a babe, lonely as hell and desperate to get back to Bali. He told me that every night he went to the pub for some company, but it was always the same weather-fucked faces, and so the first chance he had he flew home.

'Bu, is it hard, being married to a bule?'

'In what way? Privately, or with visas and government and things like that?'

'Well, privately I guess. Like with the cultural differences.'

She gives my question some consideration before answering. 'It was hard at first. You wouldn't think it now, but when Dennis first came here he was always angry about everything. "Why do you throw your rubbish out the bus window," he asked me, and, "How come I'm still paying twice as much for everything when I live here?" and, "Why did your neighbours have to go and sell their rice paddies, they've wrecked our view!"' She slaps the knees of her jeans, excited now. 'I told him, if you want to stay here with me, you must learn this culture, understand this culture. But don't complain. Stop complaining and getting angry over stupid things. It's just the way it is here, you just have to accept it. Begitulah saja.'

She smiles fondly.

From inside comes the siren of the kettle.

'So does he still get overcharged, like at the market and when he has to bargain at the shops?'

'Iya! All the time! He's a bule, kan?' Ibu chuckles softly. 'You know what he say to me? He say: "Meri, I already live here long time, why they keep calling me bule? My name is Dennis and I'm from Australia!"' Ibu wheezes with laughter. 'Ha, ha, but he still bule! I tell him, "You still bule"'

Her laughter is infectious.

She dabs her tears with a tissue and continues. 'Ya, it's better if I do the shopping. When we go on holiday to Bali, I say, "Dennis, you stay here in the hotel while I go shopping." As soon as they see him – wah! At once everything is more expensive. Hang on a moment Penny, I get the tea.'

She disappears inside.

I'm knackered. Don't think I'll make it through a cuppa. Maybe it's better to head back now. Dennis is already asleep, slumped soft in one of the chairs in the lounge. I join Meri in the kitchen. 'He had a big day today,' she says.

'Of course, I'm sorry for keeping you up so late.'

'Not at all, it was nice to finally talk to you. Can I drop you home?'

From the way Ibu asks the question she's hoping I'll decline. It's been a long day, and putting up with a bunch of whingeing bules has probably been exhausting.

'No, no, really it's fine. It truly isn't far.'

There's a thump in the roof. The triumphant sound of claws.

'If I get tired, I'll jump on an ojek.'

'Maybe it's too late for ojek.'

I wave away her concern.

The air is emptier than during the day. I fill my lungs, enjoying the brisk burn of it. On either side of the road there's the wet suck and burble of evening rice paddies. It takes me nearly an hour to walk back into Batu Batur and across town to Ibu Ayu's. I didn't realise how far out of town Dennis' village actually is. I don't feel unsafe, but consciously avoid thinking about dukuns and black magic. It's one thing to be excited about a potential trip to a dukun in the well-lit company of friends, another to entertain such a thought on a dark walk home.

Ibu Ayu's is tucked in right at the end of a lane that twists like a shoestring. During the day it's filled with big-eyed schoolkids crunching lollies and men wheeling kaki lima of sugary crushed ice. But now, the warungs and shops, all boarded shut, look completely different. A light bulb barely burns the edges of the dark. A rat weaves through the gutter grates by my left ankle. I keep an even pace.

And then I hear footsteps behind me.

There's a chattering sound and the tiny cymbal clash of something metallic. I focus on the kink in the lane ahead. After that, I'll be able to see the sign to Ibu Ayu's, can start hollering.

Whoever is behind me keeps pace. Not closing in, not falling back. Every now and then there's that strange chatter, like mice, or wind-up children. I round the kink and speed up. There's the sign now, hand-painted, with the blue curl of a wave. Behind me, the steady slap of rubber on cement. It's him, I think. It's the guy who was watching me in the shower. I hope and hope and hope that the gate is open.

It is. I slip through, shut and bolt it.

Then I run across the grass to my bungalow, climb the steps two at a time, and try to get a glimpse of the lane from the balcony. The wall is just a little too high. So I climb up onto the balcony railing and steady myself by curling my fingers around the roof.

There's a man standing just back from the gate. The fire-flower of his cigarette end blooms and fades. It's too dark to see his face. Wound around his hand is a chain. My eyes follow its straining links to a collar. A monkey's collar. The monkey looks around, alert, ears pricked. Then it slides a mask over its face and jumps onto the man's shoulder.

The man stays like that, perfectly still, face upturned.

36

I'm in tight jeans, gripping Matt between my thighs. We lock hard around a mountain corner and my breath catches. The vegetation becomes thicker as we climb: vines drop like wet lassoes, poisonous flowers exhale. There are no people, no wooden stands of durian or banana by the roadside.

At last we come to a clearing where Matt parks the bike. It's cool. Above us, birds wail long and lustily. Matt takes my hand and we walk up a dirt track. Ten minutes later, the jungle falls back around a string of steaming volcanic pools. Water trims off into water.

Matt's stripping, and my gaze whips back to his body, a bit skinny from too much surfing and rice, but not bad.

'Jesus, Pen!'

I cover my face and laugh – a moment later he's dragging my jeans over my thighs, grabbing my chin between his fingers, owning my mouth. Monkeys backfire through the trees. We fall into one of the pools. Once or twice I glance at the surrounding jungle. Matt murmurs, 'Don't worry. The locals don't come here, they're scared of the spirits.'

And so I stop looking and let those freckled lips take mine.

*

Later, I dip under, hold my breath until my lungs swell blue. Burst back. Completely physical. Completely whole.

'What kind of spirits do the locals think live here?'

'The spirits of children.'

'Oh.'

'But not all the locals. Things are changing.'

'What, with religion?'

'Sure. And the influence of the West. Technology. Look at the crew using mobile phones. No-one had one five years ago. Telly too. There's only one or two families in my village with a satellite dish but everyone's saving up.'

'Mmm.' I swim over. Circle his waist with my legs. 'So what did your parents do for work in the Pacific?'

'They were missionaries.'

'Really? So ... what about you?'

'What about me?'

'You don't – I mean, are you religious?' He's got me worried. I'm not too fond of the whole missionary idea.

'I'm not Christian. My brothers and sisters all still go to church but I was the black sheep in the family. I wouldn't say I'm *irreligious*. I'm really interested in the beliefs of the people here. Like about this place,' he presses me closer to him, 'or the place you talked about near Cahyati's village, or dukuns.'

Since last night my head has been buzzing with questions for Matt about the dukun.

'Why have you got it in for Shane? Why are you going to a dukun about him?'

Matt unlaces my legs. 'It wasn't my idea. Bapak Joni talked to me about it – he's got personal reasons for disliking Shane, and on a purely professional level, I think he's keen to take out the competition. I'm just going along for the ride, you know, interested to learn a bit more about black magic, if it can work on a bule. This kind of stuff is vanishing as quick as satellite dishes are going up.'

I tread water, perplexed. Just going along for the ride? 'But what if it does work? If Shane gets really crook and dies or something? Have you got it in for him that bad?'

'I'm not trying to kill the bloke, if that's what you're implying. But I do think he's a waste of oxygen. Like I said last night, the dukun's spell is just to make him crook, to take him out of the equation for a while. If he goes, things will be a lot easier for the rest of us who are trying to live here. There have been rumours that some of the local blokes have something else planned for him, but I don't have a clue what.'

I feel a tremor of wariness. I am certain Matt's a hell-man, one of those characters who'll be talked about across the archipelago for years to come, and like all hell-men, he courts darkness.

'So you said you wanted to go to the dukun?' There's a tilting, half-teasing, half-mad look in his eyes.

I did yesterday, in the warmth of Dennis and Meri's kitchen, mouth full of sticky rice, heart ready for adventure. But wouldn't that make me responsible, implicated, accessory to anything that happened to Shane?

'Come on then,' he says and it's a dare. A challenge.

Moral reluctance battles curiosity. Curiosity wins. But only after I've promised myself to tell Shane.

So I step out of the pool with my back to him, conscious of the water streaming from me, conscious of my own lissom body from too many bad nasi campurs and gutter-grown prawns. I wonder what he sees when he looks at me? My skin's darker than it was in Perth. My eyes are dark. My hair's long, printed straight down my back like monsoonal rain. Pretty much as good as it gets. I turn to face him. He sweeps back his hair with a hand.

'Ayo,' he says.

37

I heard a savage story about a dukun when I was a teenager. Dad had offered our house in Kuta to some family friends for a week during school holidays and we relocated to Balangan, a white-sand, blue-water cove. The road down to Balangan was still unmarked, a hazardous slide of loose gravel and slyly squealing pigs. We slept on the balcony of a guesthouse, on thin mattresses under mozzie nets. At night, Dad got on the piss and I let a Brazilian butterfly-kiss my thighs in swap for sips of buttery arak. Until I got caught. Dad was disgusted. Not because he found me necking a bloke ten years my senior but because I was with a Brazilian.

'No Germans, no Brazilians,' he told me.

'What about Japs?'

'Yeah. Japs are alright.'

Dad's measure of a man's worth was how courteous he was in the surf and how well he surfed; in his experience, Germans or Brazos didn't make the grade.

Dad kept me closer after that. No sneaking to the other guesthouses to watch the backpackers practise fire poi. No drifting to the rock platform between Balangan and Dreamland in a white dress.

The night I heard the dukun story I was wrecked sideways in a hammock. The surf had been a solid four to six foot and on low tide I missed a take-off and got dragged over a jungle of reef.

It scissored up my bikini, my back.

The blokes at the guesthouse, Aussies mostly, made a fuss and painted me up with Mercurochrome. They complimented Dad on having such a gutsy daughter and I think he was secretly proud.

With nightfall came violent rumbles. The surf was doubling, trebling. I was glad I wouldn't be able to go out the next day. The men's voices, scarred and rough, were almost crushed by the sound of the water. They were talking about Nias. One of the older men said he'd been in Nias in the '60s. With another bloke and a French girl. The three were camping out near a wave. After they'd been there a few days an old man approached and told them to leave.

'Does someone own this land? We're happy to pay,' offered the Aussie bloke.

'I don't want your money, I want you to leave.'

There was a splinter-sharp madness. A betel-tinged absence. He shuffled off.

In the surf they learnt he was the town's dukun.

They'd heard about dukuns. They weren't scared. But that night in the tent they discussed whether there'd be repercussions if they stayed.

'Nah fuck it, we'll be right.'

The next day the two men scored Lagundris. A flawless, almond-eye barrel. They surfed until they were ravenous, until their skin glowed with the wattage of Jakartan brothels. When they got in, the French girl was out, off somewhere, probably walking. That evening she still hadn't come back. All her stuff was there: passport, money, clothes. But no girl.

They never found her.

38

We follow the track further up into the mountains. The air here seems so pure compared to the air in Indonesia's cities. When you step from air-conditioning onto a pumping artery of Jakarta or Denpasar or Balikpapan it crushes you; the air's bronchial, it's infection, it's smoke and soap and shit. But here, these soaring, scarred trees keep it clean; have swallowed penicillin, the radio, and Sukarno in their rings.

After another half an hour, we reach a village and Matt pulls up in the shade. Within moments we're surrounded by a bunch of women pinching and crowing. 'Who's this? Where's she from? Is this your wife?'

Matt laughs and shakes his head.

They turn to me, talking over the top of each other in Indonesian, frank and nosy.

'Matt's a good person,' they say. 'He's put two of the children in this village through primary school and he's always bringing gifts. How long have you known him? Are you going to marry him? Do you have any children?' Their hands go to my belly. 'How long have you been in Indonesia? What hair!' They lift it out, let it run through their fingers.

We break away from the women and follow a track further into the jungle. The dukun's shack is a squat wooden structure with smoke leaking through the roof. Around it, a yard is pegged out neatly in bamboo. A couple of bare-bummed kids chase the chooks. Shell-shaped leaves spiral to rest. The dukun is nothing like I imagined, no mask or bones through his ears. He looks like an ordinary village bloke, crouching on the doorstep of his shack, mobile phone jammed between shoulder and ear, fingers racing the skin off a rambutan. He doesn't stop talking when we arrive, so Matt and I drift to a bamboo bench and wait.

'Is he the closest dukun to Batu Batur?'

'Nah, there's a couple of others in town. But Bapak Joni told me they're frauds. Their ilmu isn't very strong and the local people will only go to them if they need help to find something they've lost, or maybe if they get sick.'

My eyes are fixed on the scrimshaw patterns of ants and earth.

'Apparently his father was really powerful. People would come to him from as far away as Bandar Lampung. They say he could turn himself into a tiger, disappear. Bapak Joni reckons there's not many of them who can do that now. He told me a story about one dukun who was locked up during Dutch colonial times. Apparently this dukun could project his body so that he appeared in two places at once – both in the village and the jail. The Dutch were so spooked they let him go.'

'So has this guy's knowledge been passed down from his father?'

'Yeah, as far as I understand it's generally in the family. Usually it gets passed on to the first son but this guy is the second son. When his dad started teaching his older brother, the kid got really crook. This shit's dangerous, Penny. You've gotta be strong. You're trafficking energy from fuck knows where and if you're not strong enough ...'

A shadow eclipses the patterns of the ants.

'Penny, Bapak Dudi.' Matt stands.

The dukun holds my fingers for a moment longer than polite. Matt and the dukun speak to each other in Bahasa Lampung.

The dukun seems pissed off we're here unannounced. But when Matt pulls out a wad of fifties his eyes light up like bee stings and he quickly ushers us inside and clears space for us to sit. A ray of wet shimmering light strikes the dukun's cheekbone. In it swirls mosquito wings and dust motes. The dukun moves around the shack gathering things and I try not to breathe. The air is bitter with pond-grown vegetables.

At last the dukun settles. Marks a circle on the floor of his hut with rice. Inside the circle he places squares of paper patterned with Arabic prayers, tiny hooked bones, wire, rusty nails, chipped mirror and flinders of glass. He gestures for Matt to pass him something. It's hair. Hair the yellow of nicotine-brushed teeth. It looks like Shane's. How the hell had Matt managed to get hold of Shane's hair? The dukun's lips move but I can't understand the words. My legs ache and I uncross them. Despite crouching, Matt still doesn't seem uncomfortable. His eyes are closed, his face motionless.

Then, almost imperceptibly, the temperature changes, like the first stirrings of fever. It gets warmer and warmer. At first I think it's because there are three of us crammed into a small space, that it's the poor ventilation, but the heat builds steadily electric until even the dukun is sweating, until I feel a crushing pressure in my head like a tropical hangover no amount of Nurofen will numb.

Then blackness.

Then I'm mumbling goodnight to Matt at Ibu Ayu's, fatigued beyond belief. I don't remember what else happened in the shack. I don't remember the ride home. Think, I say to myself, twisting hot on the bed, *think*! It must be in there somewhere.

But I can't think, can't remember a thing.

39

I wake up nauseous under the beak-like click of the fan, check my phone. There's still no message from Josh. So I call him. I figure it's better this way, better to be spontaneous and heartfelt than to think and overthink what I should say.

He doesn't answer.

So I text: U ok? We need to talk.

Should I sign off with a kiss? Maybe not ...

Head whirring, I fall back onto the pillow. What on earth happened yesterday? Did Matt black out as well? He mustn't have, if he managed to ride me home. Maybe I passed out from the heat. Maybe I'm getting crook, my guts aren't a hundred percent this morning. But I've never passed out like that before, never had hours blanked out in my memory – except after heavy drinking. I'll drop in on Matt tomorrow, on the way to Shane's, will try to catch him before he heads up to Lampung for work, ask him what he remembers. I'm pretty sure he's off tomorrow. At Dennis' he said he had to go back in a couple of days.

The light in the bungalow shifts from a sun-kissed wood colour to glazed ceramic greens. Outside, a bouquet of fresh rain. Shane's tomorrow. I'm ready to start work, ready for rhythm and routine and a challenge. I wonder what he'll get me doing, if I'll be on the books as well as running the staff. That Kristi is gunna be a tough one to manage, saucy and haughty. Then the blokes who made me pay for parking – there'll be no more of *that* from tomorrow. And he's sure to have cleaning and kitchen staff, gardeners. I don't think I'm out of my depth: the budgets don't scare me, the management aspect doesn't scare me, Shane doesn't scare me, the stalking thing is uncomfortable but should ease off once I get set up with a bike. The only thing that has got me really worried is this talk about Shane being targeted, by Matt and maybe by other blokes, or young religious fanatics. Can I risk it? Is a good wage and five grand enough? Should I head to the Kiwi's and spend a day trawling for jobs, find something else, maybe in Java? I'm not going back to Perth. Not yet. Risk always makes things sharper, throws into contrast the highs and lows, gives clarity. As a surfer, I know this, I've lived this. Living in Perth, like a sleepwalker, I've missed this.

Shane's tomorrow.

40

That evening, I wait with a drink on the balcony while Ibu cooks for the Frenchman and me. It's the first time I've seen him in days. He turns the beer-curled pages of an old *Tracks* magazine. A mozzie coil poisons the cuts on our ankles.

'How much longer you here for, Emile?'

'How much?'

'When do you leave?'

Ibu Ayu shuffles out slowly with our cutlery.

'Ah. Tomorrow I think. I get the bus to mountains and then Padang.'

'You leaving already? Where you go?' Ibu Ayu asks.

'Padang. Then fly to Jakarta, Bali.'

'Oh yeah. What have you got planned in Bali?' I take a swing on my beer.

'Surfing, of course. But also yoga. There is one very famous yogi in Ubud next week. I go to him.'

'Have you got any more work lined up in the new year, any more photo stories?'

He looks at me. He's so self-contained, gives so little away. Plenty of travellers who've been on the road alone for months or years can't shut up about their experiences. The Frenchman is the exact opposite. He drops his criminally dark eyes. Turns another page.

'Maybe Burma,' he says. 'You have email?'

'Sure.'

He tears a corner from *Tracks*, scraps around for a pen.

I jot down my email address and slide it back to him, just as Ibu reappears with towers of nasi goreng ayam. You can't get any simpler than chicken fried rice but somehow it just never tastes the same when you try to cook it at home. Probably the MSG. I tally up another beer. Ibu hovers over the table. 'Penny, when you leave?'

'Tomorrow,' I say through a mouthful of rice. 'I'm pretty keen to see Matt on the way but still don't know where he lives. Could you draw me a map?'

'What do you want, going to Matt's village?' Ibu asks bluntly.

I don't want to tell her about the dukun.

'Just because,' I say with a shrug.

She grumbles for a bit then accepts the Frenchman's offer of *Tracks* and a pen. While she's drawing over an advertisement for wetsuits I ask about Cahyati.

'Is she here, Bu? I'd love to see her before I head off.'

'She busy at the moment,' Ibu says shortly. 'Nah, already finish.' She pushes the map toward me and explains how to get to Matt's. Then she stands. 'Okay. I get the bills ready now so you don't forget.'

Emile and I share a smile then go back to our rice.

41

I click through the gears in a pair of heels. No helmet. Hair snarled and wild over my shoulders. I rented the motorbike from Ibu this morning to get out to Shane's. My heart is full, racing; there're snatches of song on my lips. I'm stoked to be catching Matt, stoked to be starting work, stoked that the sun is out, that it's still cool.

Matt's village consists of a few streets of wooden houses on stilts. The houses have wide sagging balconies and roofs like upturned boats. His house is the furthest out toward the mountains. Through the jade shimmer of morning the mountains look as though they could dissolve.

Matt's working in the front yard, his sexy sun-trashed body naked to the waist. He's planting something, turning the earth in his hands. A woman appears at the door. I pull up in the shade of a banana plant. Neither of them has noticed me. He's stretching to stand, is turning to her.

She's stunning. In a finely woven sarong with high to-die-for cheekbones and an uncovered sweep of hair; hair that would delight Indian hair thieves and black American weave artists. Matt enfolds her – she's tiny in his arms – and he spreads his hands over her belly. She's obviously, glowingly pregnant.

I clench the handlebars of my motorbike until my knuckles turn a wishbone white. I want to burn straight to Shane's. Obliterate myself with Bintangs. Obliterate the shock opening black in my chest. A blackness, blankness far worse than even yesterday's forgetting. But I can't move. I'm spellbound, watching Matt's woman.

The sun has just come out. It catches in her hair. Sends copper shimmers through it. Her perfect chin is lifted to Matt and her face glows. How could I compete with such an effortlessly trim and submissively soft-eyed village girl? I can't – don't want to. Looking at the way she gazes at him, I regret ever meeting him.

He looks up. And sees me.

'Penny.' A steel-hard drawl.

I give the motorbike handle a Chinese burn and jump from the shade of the banana tree.

Slide to a stop on the other side of the fence.

'Matt.'

There's a vicious smell of rotting bananas and water spinach.

'What are you doing here?'

'I...' I can't bear to meet his eyes. 'I was just on the way to Shane's.'

'You shouldn't be here.'

You shouldn't have fucked me when you've got a pregnant partner.

The girl looks at me curiously, lingeringly, her head cocked to one side.

Matt says something to her in Bahasa Lampung and she turns and sways back toward the house.

'So?' His mouth has a firm, sour set. A Javanese sarong hangs from his hips, an intricate print in earthy browns.

I can't remember why I'm here. I've made an unforgivable trespass and we'll never be lovers again.

'You've got some fucken cheek,' he moves hard up against the fence and I finally raise my eyes to his. There's nothing in them that's recognisable, nothing to hold on to.

And then she's back, slipping out through the sarong-covered door. Matt turns. She's carrying a tray toward us, loaded up with two cups of black tea.

'Teh dulu.'

'No,' I say quickly, kicking the bike into first. 'No thank you.'

42

Goats flee. Children scream. The sky aches with rain. I flog the bike. Overtake a truck and speed headlong toward a 4WD with a hundred surfboards strapped to the roof. Pink and black and army-patterned board bags. A Sumatran at the wheel. Impassive. Smoking a kretek. He probably accelerates. There's a bule in the passenger seat next to him. Probably Australian. Probably whitening under smudges of skin cancer. I swerve in front of the truck at the last minute. The palms snap shut. Clouds lock out the sun. And then the rain comes. Rain that falls so hard the rice paddies smoke. Rain that churns the road giardial. I twist the throttle until I can't twist it any further. Make Shane's in record time.

There's no-one lingering in the car park, no-one guarding the bikes or filching rupiahs. Through a trough in the trees, along the river, I can hear the ocean, unseasonably loud. I knock on the door. There's no answer. I knock again. When there's still no answer I open it and walk through.

Kristi meets me on the deck. Her eyes are small and hard as papaya seeds. 'Terlambat.' You're late. She looks me up and down. 'And wet. Shane tell me to show you the room.'

She leads me to a room with six single beds in it, obviously the dorm Shane mentioned the other night and no doubt their windowless worst. I'm surprised he even offers a dorm. Probably just covering all bases.

'Shared kamar mandi.'

'No way.' I distinctly remember Shane saying I could have my pick of the rooms, just not one of the bungalows. 'I want to see the lot.'

She sizes me up for a moment, probably wondering if she'll be able to push me over. But she must find something unsympathetic in my face, some hint of the rage in my heart, because she scowls and pulls the door shut.

I choose a room further along the wooden corridor and around a corner. It's spacious, with air-con, a television, a double bed and big windows full of palm shadows. In the bathroom there's a Western-style toilet and a shower that smells strongly of disinfectant. On the whitewashed walls are two cheaply framed photos of the right-hand wave out the front. It doesn't have the same romance as Ibu Ayu's bungalows. In fact, it's completely soulless.

'Shane wants to see you as soon as you're ready,' she says. Then she sniffs and saunters off.

I tear my clothes from my bag and swear. Everything is soaked after the motorbike ride. I tie up a line from the bed frame to a hook in the wall, string up my wet clothes and crank the AC. My clothes smell, not just of damp but of sweat, sharp as vinegar. Then I tidy my hair, my running makeup, and go and find Shane.

His massive forearms rest against the railing on the deck.

'Penny,' he says without turning.

'Hey Shane, how are ya?'

'You're late. By morning I didn't mean ten.'

'Sorry.'

He turns. I wonder if it's part of the dukun's spell or if he always looks this bad in the mornings. 'What the fuck happened to you? You look like a drowned rat,' he says.

My arms fold across my chest self-consciously.

'Righto then. Room's all sorted? Good. Follow me.'

He takes me to the kitchen first. 'We've only got two staff on at the moment but I'll get you training up a team before the dry kicks in. This is Tengku and Umar.'

The boys shuffle forward and shake my hand limply.

'We do a Western buffet breakfast for our guests every morning – cereals, toast, banana pancakes, omelettes, bacon.'

No way, not bacon. There's no way Shane would be that culturally insensitive. Then again, Pak Wu probably wouldn't mind supplying it for a price …

'You'll make sure all this is set up, along with tea, coffee, water,' Shane's making a list on his fingers, 'and a couple of jugs of fresh juice. As the guests arrive, take their orders, give the orders to the boys, then go and mingle, make small talk, deal with any complaints. If you need to throw in some extra Vegemite or something to keep a guest happy, whatever. Okay?'

'Don't you, I mean, don't you think it would be better, more authentic, if a local was bringing out local food?'

'Are you saying there's something wrong with my food? That you're not prepared to waitress?'

'I'm just saying maybe people have come to Indo to experience Indo.'

'They can get Indo out there,' Shane stabs a finger toward Batu Batur. 'Here, I want to create a haven, a place where people feel safe. Ideally, the kind of traveller I want staying here is someone who'll eat with us, rent motorbikes from us, use us as their transport to Bandar Lampung and back. Who needs packages. Who is on limited time. And so,' he scoops a hand around my elbow, leads me out of the kitchen and turns a corner into an air-conditioned office, 'after breakfast is wound up I want you to start working on giving me some figures. How much for a website?

How much for an ad on Magicseaweed? On Coastalwatch? In *Tracks*? How do we start marketing to this kind of traveller? So far it's been word-of-mouth and a write-up in the *Lonely Planet*. Last season I was at about sixty percent capacity. It's time to step it up. You've got the internet here, it's slow, but it works, and so in two weeks time I want you to deliver me a budget and a marketing plan.'

'Got it.'

'In the arvo you can have a break for a few hours. Go surfing, to town, whatever. Your business. Then, from six pm until late, you're on the bar. I want you to make sure the beer fridge is always stocked and that the beers are icy. And I want you to try any spirits you're unfamiliar with. There is nothing worse than having staff who don't drink serving alcohol. A constant problem here. How the fuck can you know if a drink is good if you've never tasted it?'

'Agreed.'

'Any questions?'

There's no pretense of chumminess, no hint of flirtation: he's brusque, businesslike, and it suits me fine.

'What about Kristi, what's her job?'

'We've just lost the girl from housekeeping, so she's back on cleaning duties.'

Shit. She was on the bar last time I was here. There'll be trouble for sure.

'Does she answer to me?' I ask.

'No. Kristi answers to me. And you'll answer to me too. I'll be roping you in to all sorts of jobs. Tour-guiding, translating, organising onward tickets for guests. But most importantly, like I said before, you need to be bringing in customers, essentially paying your own wage with the business you bring in. Now, any other questions?'

'Those guys who guard the motorbikes.' I pause, waiting for Shane to indicate recognition.

'What guys?'

'The ones who charged me for parking last time I was here.'

'You serious? I don't pay anyone to look after the bikes. Do you remember what they looked like?'

I shake my head.

'Well, it's probably not a bad idea,' Shane says, half to himself. Then he gestures to the computer. 'Get to work.'

43

The boys whip me up a nasi goreng when I knock off. The morning was busy. I barely thought about Matt and didn't even stop for lunch. Now, with a full belly under the AC in my room, I feel a rush of shame, and of stupidity at being tricked. At least Matt won't be around town for the next couple of weeks. And even after that, it sounds like Shane wants me working at well above the normal tropical pace, so I probably won't get much free time at all.

My mind wanders back to the dukun's, to the strange collection of objects he placed in the circle of rice: prayers, bones, glass, hair. Matt was completely absorbed by the ceremony and it gets me thinking that to live here, to really live here harmoniously, it's almost like you have to unlearn everything you know. Starting with a physical unlearning. The first bad nasi campur and you come unravelled. It's only after hitting battery acid bile that you can start to reweave your resistance, unpick and re-stitch. Sickness is never just physical. There're the mental battles, trying to move limbs antagonised with inertia, the frustration of endless, unproductive hours, the loneliness of not speaking your own tongue and that mocking and trenchant question: why are you doing this to yourself? To live here, toughening up physically and toughening up mentally to deal with the constant physical stress – the malaria, the dengue, the gut-bugs, the moisture-sucking heat – are only the first steps. And then what next? It's like Meri said. At some point you have to stop fighting. You have to let go of everything that frustrates and infuriates. Every person who throws a plastic bottle over a ferry railing, every person who rips you off on the bus or at the market, every time someone elbows you aside at the checkout, or ignores you if you're with a man. You have to let it go otherwise you get ground down, come undone ...

Just as I'm falling asleep, my phone vibrates. There's a message from Josh. The message says: Wait for me.

What the hell does that mean?

44

The following day I knock off at three thirty, hit the beach. A group of fishermen are crouched over a net. They look up, kreteks blazing in the corners of their mouths.

'Hello Mister,' says one, fingers dancing.

'Sore,' I answer.

'Sore!' comes a chorus, this time with smiles. 'Dari mana Bu?' Where are you from?

One of the bolder fishermen looks at me from under a faded baseball cap. 'Dari Amerika?' he guesses.

America? I feign horror. 'Nggak. Australia!'

'Ohhh, Australiiii!'

His fingers keep moving.

'Sudah bisa berbahasa Indonesia, ya?'

'Iya.'

The man asks me the usual questions in Indonesian, then the conversation takes a troubling turn.

'Is it true,' the fisherman asks, 'is it true there's free sex in Australia? Sex bebas?'

'What do you mean?'

I've been asked this question plenty of times and still have no idea how to answer truthfully. But something serious is at stake here, perhaps the reception of every female tourist at Shane's from today onward.

'Well,' says the fisherman, 'there are always tourists at Shane's.

Mainly young guys. But sometimes they come with their girlfriends and they sleep in the same room together, even though they're not married. So they're having sex aren't they? Sleeping in the same room? Like free sex!'

The rest of the men look at me expectantly.

'Pak, nothing is free.'

The men snigger, they know about maintenance.

But baseball cap isn't so easily placated. 'How many boyfriends have you had?' he insists.

What a question! What can I say? Fifteen. Twenty. I've lost count. Sometimes there are things you can't explain. Cultural differences so vast you don't know where to start.

'Different cultures yeah, Pak,' I say as a final cop-out.

They start to murmur to each other and then one of them shouts and points to the sea. A boat glides toward us through the channel. The men on the boat wait for the shore break to lull, then ease it through a crack in the flat, barely submerged rock shelf. The shelf is probably studded with sea urchins. Pig's bristles. Not a good spot for a dip before work this evening. The fishermen drop the net and run to help lift the boat up the sand and in line with the other fishing boats. They're all painted blue. What happens when the winter swells sweep in, when the ocean is blind muscle in June, July, August? Do the men still go fishing? What happens if or when the channel between the two waves closes out? Do many fishermen drown? Can they swim? The men unload the catch and start to head up tracks under the coconut palms: to their wives, to their shacks, to the fish market. I catch the man with the baseball cap before he disappears.

'Pak! Pak! Maaf ya, menganggu lagi.' Sorry for disturbing you again!

'Nggak apa.' He peers hard at me.

'Has Shane banned you from launching your boats through this channel?'

The fisherman's face, already dark with sun and scuppered by sea, darkens further. He's weighing something up. Deciding whether he can trust me.

'He wants us to pay a tax,' he says at last. 'On what we earn from the fish.'

I wait.

He shifts his weight, uncomfortable now. 'And our daughters. He wants our daughters to be on call to work for him.'

'Are you going to pay?'

He sucks his teeth. 'Nggak.'

I don't get a chance to ask another question. There's a roar from down the beach. It's Rick, the West Australian, shirtless and wearing, in a gesture of extreme irony or extreme ignorance, a conical hat woven from pandanus leaves and worn by the poor, by farmers in rice paddies throughout Indonesia, Vietnam, Laos.

'Hey Penny!'

He wedges me in a hug and I stiffen; I don't feel intimate enough with Rick to be comfortable in a hug and it probably confirms the fisherman's skewed perspective of Western women. At last he releases me. His eyes are like two grey drills. Fervent. Hillsong.

'What are you up to?' he asks.

'Was just having a yarn to these blokes. What about yourself?'

'Just strolled down for a surf check. Don't know if I'll get in the water. Gotta sort out the insurance stuff for the villas.'

'Yeah, no doubt.'

'Always got time for a cuppa though,' he says. 'What are you doing just now?'

'Drifting.'

'I know a place that will still be open if you're keen.'

I can't think of anything worse than spending my lunch break with Rick. But no doubt we'll be running in to each other regularly and so I tell him sure, sure, I'm keen.

45

Whoever set up Roger's Cafe has tapped into a niche market. If tourists keep coming to Batu Batur, they'll make a killing. We're high up enough so that the view over the Indian Ocean is staggering – you could sink into a chair on the deck and watch that view forever, never tire, watch the ocean as it boils blue and folds white, watch as it dices a thousand tropical suns to pieces. Inside are cushions and beanbags and stacks of surfing magazines. The menu is vegetarian and the coffees aren't packet pre-mixes. Actually, the coffee list is impressive: beans from Aceh, Toraja, Java – and a choice of cardamom- or vanilla-infused milk. I wonder if it will be as good as the list promises. Although I noticed the sign from the road, I never thought to come up and check it out. Why didn't Ibu Ayu spruik it? Those three grungy backpackers who rolled through Ayu's would've known about it. They were probably having tofu burgers and vanilla coffees here everyday. It must be in the *Lonely Planet*.

There're about a dozen tourists in the cafe.

'I might just grab a coffee,' Rick says.

'I'll grab some food if that's cool, I haven't had anything since breakfast.'

We sit outside. Beside us, two Germans order.

'I will take the cappuccino.'

The waitress jots it down.

'And I would like the freshly pressed orange juice. Freshly

pressed. No, no, no. *Not* from the bottle! *Freshly pressed.* Do you understand?'

She comes to us next.

'Boleh minta kopi vanilla. Dan bihun goreng.'

'I'll have a long black, thanks,' says Rick.

His eyes follow the waitress' bum – it's jacked up tight in jeans. Then they swing back to me.

'So you speak a bit of Indo, hey?'

'Yeah. Yourself?'

Rick spreads his hands and when he smiles, dimples flower on his cheeks. He might charm cheerleaders or the girls at his church but I'm unimpressed.

'The whole world speaks English. Why would I bother learning Indo?'

I look at my nails. The polish has lifted in bubbles.

Rick lets his hands fall.

Below us, rice paddies are arranged in perfect squares.

The waitress breaks the tension by setting down our coffees. When she leaves, Rick asks, 'So what do you think of Indonesian guys? Do you find them attractive?'

'Indonesian guys?'

It's been a morning of unexpected, too-close-for-comfort questions.

'Indonesian *guys*?' I repeat. 'I guess it's like anywhere. There's good-looking blokes, there's average-looking blokes.' Once again, Rick's assuming an intimacy I'm not comfortable with. I change the subject. 'Do you think the local crew are gunna try and wreck your villas again?'

'I won't give 'em a chance. No way,' Rick blows across his long black.

'What about Shane, do you reckon he's safe?'

'None of us are. Not at the moment. But it's inevitable.

Development of the area. Look at Bali, no – look at Ibu Ayu and Bapak Joni's business. They've got the right idea. Embrace development. Change with it. They've seen the light. Dollars speak louder than anything else in this country.'

I take a sip of my coffee. Black flecks of vanilla dust the foam. I place it reverently back in its saucer. It's the best coffee I have ever tasted. 'Do dollars speak louder than religion, do you think? What about when the local crew are out of pocket, like with the fishermen? Can you believe this, Shane even wants to put *a tax* on them, and –'

Rick interrupts, 'Looks like your noodles are here.'

I look at him, uncomprehending for a moment. Then exasperated, I give up. What a jerk.

He tries to engage me in frivolous conversation but I grunt monosyllabic answers, concentrate on polishing off my noodles. 'I probably should go back to Shane's. I'm on the bar tonight,' I say through a mouthful.

'I'll take you past my villas on the way. There's something I want to show you.'

Given that Rick's riding, I don't have a choice.

46

On the way down the hill we pass two young men rattling a plastic bucket in the middle of the road. They're gathering money for one of the local mosques. The motorbike in front of us slows and the rider reaches into his bag for some coins.

Rick accelerates, gets on the horn. 'Fucken terrorists. That's where it starts, Penny.'

I wish I had a spare thousand rupiah but I'd left a tip with lunch and now only have big notes. On principle I don't donate to religious organisations, but it would be worth it to see Rick's reaction.

A bit further on Rick pulls over beside a rack lined with golden bottles. We climb off and wait as a woman fills his motorbike. The petrol stand is positioned in front of a shop selling the usual collection of soaps, sweets, razors and tissues. In front of it, on a low wooden bench, sits an old man with a cane. The man's eyes are like fermented milk. Two schoolboys torment him. The smaller of the boys is content to tap the man's shoulder then scamper away. The older of the boys is more malicious, twisting the old man's skin in a pinch. The old man looks humiliated, furious; he turns his head from side to side to catch the sound of their receding footfalls, their cruel giggles. Rick jumps in first.

'Oi, you little faggots, cut it out!'

They understand his tone.

For a moment, Rick is redeemed.

For a moment, the old man and the schoolboys face us, their pantomime suspended, and then the old man asks the boys slowly, 'Who was that?'

'Bule,' spits the older kid.

'Bule?' confirms the old man.

And then it shifts. It becomes them and us. The old man's face realigns in a mask of resentment.

Rick doesn't notice. He's swinging the bike around, jaw set hard. I climb on behind him and we take off. Five minutes down the road we pass a sign on the left reading Paradise Villas but we don't turn, we keep going.

'Wasn't that it?' I yell in his ear.

'Yeah. But I said I wanted to show you something.'

We take the next left. The road is ulcered with holes. Just when I'm starting to get tremors of pain up my back he kills the engine.

'Jump off,' he whispers.

We creep for about a hundred metres further along the road then crouch behind a screen of palms.

'See!' Rick stabs a finger. '*That's* what it's like trying to get anything done here.'

We're at the back of the construction site. Four blokes are curled up like cats in squares of shadow. They have cast their tools around them and are sleeping, or lying so still as to appear asleep.

Rick takes note.

'Red, checkers, black, green,' he mutters to himself.

'What's with the colours?'

'Colours of their shirts. So I know which ones to fire first. Their faces all look the same. It's just to prove a point, really, because in a week I'm gunna lay off the lot of them. Bring in a bunch of Javos to finish the job. The people here are too difficult.'

Always asking for more money, always making demands, always out to rip me off. They're real savages compared to the Javos.'

It's the stupidest thing I've heard. His construction site has already been targeted once. Sacking his current employees will only create further hostility. He'll be lucky to get the bungalows finished at all.

I follow him back to the bike and this time we approach the villas from the front.

From this angle the construction site is a frenzied hive. There are blokes welding in sunnies, using nail guns in thongs. A couple of open drums are being used to heat tar.

'I tell ya,' Rick starts to say as he walks to the closest villa-in-progress, 'the biggest drama I've had has been over the cost of materials. Get this – for the past eight months, if I gave my site manager say, one hundred thousand rupiah to buy wood or washers or whatever, only fifty thousand rupiah of that was being spent on materials. He was getting his mates in the shops to dodgy the receipts and pocketing the rest. See, they look at you and think, you're white, you're a bule, you don't know how things work here and you're not gunna stand up to them if you find out. Wrong. I've been kicking around long enough to have contacts in high places.'

We veer around to the back of the villas and now, there are no slouchers in sight.

Red, checkers, black, green.

'So I told my site manager, listen mate, I can –' he clicks his fingers, 'and have men in a black limousine with machine guns here tomorrow.'

I'm disgusted beyond the point of responding.

'Bastard still owes me six million rupes! Corruption, mate, it's everywhere.' Then Rick catches a glimpse of a green shirt and is off.

I can't stomach the thought of watching him fire the bloke. 'Hey Rick! I'll catch you later!'

He looks over his shoulder and those mad-warm eyes peel me. 'Sure Penny, it was really nice talking to you. *Really* nice.'

Tongue-trills and whistles follow me down the road.

47

It's interesting to observe the way power animates a person, how it swells the chest, deepens the voice, hardens the handshake. Perhaps power, not politics, is the art of controlling your environment. Right now, Shane's a chilling portrait of power. Tengku, Umar and Kristi are seated submissively at a table while he towers over them, arms folded in a way that accentuates the bulge of his muscles. He's delivering instructions, fast and direct, but breaks off mid-sentence when he sees me.

'Penny. Here. Now.'

I sit down next to Kristi.

'I was just saying, day after tomorrow, I'm heading to Medan. I won't be away long, just until the end of the week, but while I'm gone, someone needs to be here all the time. Do you understand me? The place is not to be left empty. Now, do we remember what happened last time I went away?'

He hasn't had his first drink for the night and his tone is mean, like a single blade razor catching unsoaped skin.

'Kristi, tell Penny what happened last time I went away.'

Kristi is silent.

An interrogative white light pools on the table between us.

'Well?'

Kristi stays silent. She looks so young: no breasts, no stomach, just those bruised Modigliani eyes.

I can't bear the tension, can't bear the soft rain of fear in my chest, can't bear how he's trying to shame her. It's not too unusual for something like this to happen in the workplace at home but things are done differently here. You never shame people in front of their colleagues. Shane's doing this for my benefit.

'Well,' I break the silence, 'whatever it was, it's not gunna happen this time. Is it guys?' Tengku and Umar offer no support; they're absorbed by their hands. 'Don't worry about it, Shane. We'll be right. Have you got a number we can call you on while you're away, you know, in case anything –'

'Did I *ask* you to speak for me?' Kristi darts me a vicious look.

'Oh, for fuck's sake,' Shane says. 'Grow up. You three, fuck off. Penny, get me a rum and get yourself a drink too. I'll tell ya what happened myself.'

Shane relocates to a chair at the edge of the balcony and I'm careful not to spill a drop as I pass him his rum.

I settle into the chair next to him, half-moons of sweat under my boobs.

'Sorry to put you through that,' he says, and his tone has completely changed. He sounds sincerely sorry. He sounds sincerely warm. 'I've gotta come down hard on them, or they'll take me for a ride. Even the girl. Especially the girl. So, you reckon you can do it?'

'Sure.' I don't know if he's referring to the job or to keeping an eye on the place while he's away but I can do it, whatever it is, I can do it.

'Good.'

Over to our left, there's a sob of wind up the river.

When he starts talking, I expect to hear the story Kristi refused to tell but instead he asks, 'You hear about the church they bombed in Padang last week?'

'The church? No, I didn't hear anything.'

In this light, his wrinkle lines intensify the angular quality of his face. He's very handsome. 'I need you to be onto it,' he says. 'I need you to be aware of what's going on across the country – especially stories of this kind. Things that are happening nationally might affect us locally.'

'Sure. So what was the go with the church in Padang?' Padang's not too far down the road.

'Well, predictably, from what I hear, the local police haven't been too forthcoming with details. Plenty of the politicians are sympathetic too – no doubt they're protecting the radical mob responsible. But it really comes down to the communities. The communities here are becoming more and more hostile.'

'Is it really that bad?' I'd always been impressed by Indo's pluralism – especially in Bali – even if it is, to a degree, superficial. The side-by-side blue and white signs indicating a nearby mosque, a temple, a church; the bars and cafes staffed by kids of all faiths, from all over the archipelago.

'Are you kidding?' His tone's blistering. 'There's been a bunch of cases where building licences for churches have been revoked or simply not given at all. And did you know most Indos would prefer not to live next door to someone of a different faith? I've been in Indo for over thirty years now. Believe me, I've seen this place change. Even in Aceh – well, I guess Aceh has always been more conservative – but it's still changing, and not for the fucken better.'

'So where's the change coming from, I mean, does it start in the villages with a few radical imams, or is this shift being driven by people in the cities?'

'What is this, the fucken *7.30 Report*?' There's no sting; the rum's relaxed him. 'Look, I couldn't really tell you. But as long as corruption continues politically, as long as poverty continues socially, these Islamic groups will get stronger and stronger. Elements of Sharia law are being adopted all over the place.

We're gunna see more bombings, we're gunna see beheadings, and we're gunna see things a whole lot more difficult for us bules living in Muslim backwaters like Batu Batur. Jesus, they might even ban this,' he gestures to the last of my rum.

I throw it back.

Hear the sea somewhere below, churning tissues and turds.

48

With the afternoon light dashing orange through the window, I put the finishing touches on a marketing plan and budget for Shane. Provided no guests turn up, the next three days should be pretty low-key. My head's swimming with sugar from the morning's coffees and I'm ready to head out for a few hours. Tengku and Umar are crunched over a chessboard on the dining deck and barely look at me as I leave.

Given the limited Indo tucker on Shane's menu I'm keen to see if there are any warungs nearby. I'd also like a place to go that's not Shane's – it's difficult when you live where you work, especially if you don't have an escape, somewhere you can switch off.

There are no fishermen on the beach, no surfers on the wave. While Shane's away this has to be the perfect time to get in the water. Although the right's a dry-season wave, on thick, windless afternoons like this, it's definitely surfable. It'd be nice to get a feel for it before the season really starts, before the carloads of Aussies pour in, charged up on steroids and bravado, adrenaline and ego.

With thongs slipping, I walk toward the maze of rat tracks that plait through the trees and pick one. The track leads past a straggle of salt-chewed wooden homes and after a few minutes, opens onto a village square. The square is shaded by an enormous tree, a king of a tree, the archetypal tree: the kind to inspire worship, awe, animism. Two men crouching at its base break my reverie with an enthusiastic 'Hello Mister!' Over to my right there's a warung, window stacked with mouth-watering triangles of brown food. The woman who runs the warung is thrilled when I step inside, says I'm the first bule to ever eat here.

Just as I'm sponging up the last of a furiously spicy chicken broth a wind comes up, sudden and violent. Where moments before there were supine shadows on balconies, or people stretched out on shop floors, there's now panic. The two men crouched under the tree spring to their feet and sprint toward the warung. A kite-tail of rubbish tears across the square in front of them. The giant tree tosses, the palms bend backwards.

'Angin, Mister!' one of the men says, parking panting in the doorframe.

'Ya, angin.'

Sure there's wind. But why the panic? Across the square, women and grandmothers and fishermen are huddled under their balcony roofs, talking, squawking, superstitiously staring at the sky.

'Dari mana, Mister?' asks the man in the doorframe, stepping inside the warung so his friend can also enter. The novelty of a bule clearly outweighs the mystical, village-rousing effect of this wind. They take a seat at the table across from me. Close enough to make conversation but not close enough to intrude.

'Australia.'

'Australiii.' The first man nods knowledgeably. 'My brother in Australi. Sydney.'

'Have you been to visit?'

The man shakes his head. 'No.' He flips open a packet of kretek cigarettes. 'Rokok?'

'No thanks.'

He signals to the ibu and gruffly orders tea.

I mean to ask them about the wind, about the agitation through the village – is it simply the fear of plummeting coconuts, or something else; perhaps uneasy spirits, an angry god? But I don't get the chance. The blokes hammer me with the usual questions, blending Indonesian with a brave, stuttering English.

'You already marry?'

'Yes,' I lie.

'Where your husband?'

I wave my hand vaguely.

'How much, ticket from Australia to Indonesia?'

'Banyak dong!' Heaps!

And then: 'Keagamaan apa, Mister?' What's your religion?

Usually I don't think twice about answering Christian. I'm not Christian, but saying I am seems to arrest any further discussion. Right now though, I'm thinking of that freshly bombed church in Padang. So I tell the men I don't have a religion and predictably they become perplexed. I'm not sure if they'll press the issue, go into the whole 'if you don't believe in God then what do you believe in?' but they both seem content to leave it at that.

What I don't expect is for them to ask if I'd heard about the bombing.

'I did hear about it. Who do you think did it?'

'Jemaah Islamiyah. Don't you know Mister? Bali bomb. Before Bali bomb, JI bomb church in Jakarta, Medan, Sukabumi ... apa lagi?'

'Uh ... Mataram ...' adds the second man.

'So what do people here think about it? Could it happen here as well?'

'Maybe similar, but not the same,' says the second man.

His friend gives him an elbow.

Ibu appears with their tea, one-third sugar, two-thirds boiling water, a limp bag.

'What do you mean it could happen here?'

'Ya ...' the second man mumbles vaguely.

'Begini ya,' the first man says, 'in Padang they're a lot more ...' he hammers his fist into his hand. 'Maybe it's not just JI but also some imams and local people only want mosques, not churches. Me personally? I think mosque, church, temple, this is Indonesia, ya? Many people, many religions, why not?'

He puts his lips to his tea, sips. 'The mayor of Padang is trying to make a new rule. He wants Christian girls to wear headscarves to school.'

'And what do you think about this?'

'Lebih baik,' says the second man. Better.

Outside, the wind streaks through the palms in a long dark bruise.

Should I run for it now, or risk getting stuck in the warung for the next hour or so if it rains?

The decision is made for me.

A hot crack of thunder and sudden rain sizzling the dirt.

I settle back against the wall and order a tea.

49

My toenails are growing in, my eyebrows are flaring out: it's time to follow the Kiwi's beauty-salon mud map. It leads to a shopfront brightened with rockmelon paint and bookended by a tailor and warung. A glance at the floor almost prompts me to jump back on the bike – it's nearly invisible under a thatch of black, unswept hair. Two unoccupied chairs are turned toward oval mirrors; on the wall there's a discoloured poster of effeminate Korean guys modelling hairstyles from the '90s, all spike and sideways fringe.

'Yaaaa, mau apaaa?' A woman appears, formidably fat and girlish: pink lipstick, no headscarf, carefully straightened hair.

'Bisa mani pedi, Bu? Dan bisa waxing alis mata?'

'Ya, of course!' she enthuses.

I look again at the unswept floor, think of the last cucumber-pale flakes of burn between my legs. Then I think of the immaculately groomed Kiwi and so I let the beautician sway me, gushing and gossipy.

'What's your name? Where are you from? No children?! Oh wow. I'm Surti. Yes, I've got two, very naughty! No, no, I'm not from here, I'm from Surabaya, Jawa Timur. My husband, though, he's from here. A fisherman – see how dark he is? Too much sun!' She points to a wedding photo. He's handsome and she looks gorgeous, cinched in a traditional kebaya, a mask of makeup starching her skin. 'Ahh … Surabaya,' she sighs.

'What do you miss most? Family?'

'Ya, I miss my family a little bit.'

The cloth's barely noticeable, the quick rip, rip, rip.

'But what I really miss is the shopping malls! Have you been to Surabaya? Anything you want, you can buy in Surabaya. Cell phone, electronics, makeup. Wow! Last time I was in Surabaya I bought a handycam. You know, to make video? Very expensive, nearly one million rupiah. I used it for two weeks but then I got bored.' She pauses then her eyes brighten. 'Penny mau beli handycam? Half a million only!'

'No, no, no thanks, Surti, I don't really need a video camera.'

She murmurs understandingly, then giggles. 'Oh wow, my husband was so angry when he found out how much I paid …'

She pushes me to sitting. 'Okay, all done! You like?'

Surti's transformed caterpillars to crescent moons.

'They're perfect!'

'Really?' she's pleased. 'Now nails, ya?'

Outside, over the scrape of brooms on cement, there's the caterwaul of kids. Moments later, a boy and girl tumble through the door with fingers the colour of Burger Rings. They've both got lolly-punched teeth.

'Dik, dik, jangan nakal! Keluar!' Don't be naughty, get outside, Surti commands.

They don't. Instead, they stomp and spit and puff out their chests. Surti ignores them, deftly working the cuticle nipper. When she gets up to look for the nail scissors and her back is turned, her children move in with their orange fists and rain me with small blows. I'm saved from savaging by the song of an ice-cream man. He's walking down the lane toward us with his cart. The children's fists drop and they fly out the door. Nudging and shouldering each other, they order ice-creams. When the man asks for payment, they gesture toward the salon. Their ice-cream wrappers are already crumpled in the dirt at their feet.

Surti's missed all of this, bent over my toes, but when the ice-cream man comes to the door of the salon, explaining that she owes him money, Surti explodes. The man hangs his head and scuffs his thongs in the dust. A couple of times he lifts his chin, just long enough to snatch a look at me, then he drops them again. Finally, when she's finished giving him a serve, Surti hands over the money for the ice-creams and sends him away.

'Bodoh!' she spits when he's out of earshot. Idiot! 'Every second day this happens. Those naughty kids! I tell him again and again, don't sell them ice-cream unless they've got the money in their hand. I think he's a bit slow. Bodoh banget! It's hard, ya Penny, two naughty kids, husband always away fishing … Aduh!'

Just as she's putting the finishing touches on the polish, another two ladies come in. They glance at me briefly then ignore me, whipping off their headscarves and angling their faces at the oval mirrors. Their conversation leaps from haircuts and colours to a local woman who's always flirting with their husbands at the fish market. Have you seen the eye shadow she wears? And she's got six children already and not even twenty-five! And I saw her go to the fish market *twice* last week, on the same morning. Claimed she 'forgot' something. Forgot she had a husband, more like! Yes, well, what can you expect? She *is* from Java … Oh – sorry Surti. You know what we mean.

Sitting there, with the polish on my fingernails and toenails drying, I realise it's one of the first times on this trip I haven't felt like a spectacle. Like the bule. For a moment it feels completely normal: the children racing in and out, the vanity, the conversation which, with a few minor tweaks, could easily be an eavesdropped conversation at a beauty salon at home.

On my way out the door, just as Surti is fluffing up the first woman's hair, I hear her saying, 'So Bu, last time I was in Surabaya, I bought this handycam …'

50

Back at Shane's, Tengku, Umar and Kristi have disappeared. Their motorbikes aren't in the car park and a thorough search of the resort doesn't offer any clues. I end up in a chair outside my room thinking about the light; it's always the light that gets you first, teasing out stirrings of nostalgia or homesickness. The post-rain primaries of Fiji, the solemn-cold olives of Albany. And Indo – Indo is always slightly blurred, as if under a film of memory or longing, regardless of whether it's the wet or the dry season, whether the light is tindery or there's that smoky green wash over everything. This afternoon is no different. Although there's no view of the ocean from the balcony, there is a frieze of vegetation. Jellyfish-shaped pools of light surge through the leaves with the damp wind.

I wonder what keeps Tengku, Umar and Kristi here indefinitely, as employees. There'd be other jobs going, for cleaners, for cooks. Perhaps Shane's got them hooked, as well, on the promise of above-average wages. Good money is often enough to sideline suffering. It is for me, anyway. With the wage Shane's offering and the bonus, with the free accommodation and free food, with the reluctance to end up with Josh back in Scarborough, I'm committed to seeing the six months out. And while it's quiet now (most places are in the lead-up to Christmas) once things get going there'll be guests to keep me busy, to keep me from being roped in as Shane's nightly drinking partner.

I haven't spent enough time with him to make any definitive judgements. He's a prick, he's a real prick to his local staff, but not the kind of guy to chop off someone's fingers – it's more likely that happened in Saudi. What I do wonder is if Shane, volatile and charismatic, intelligent and crass, will be a kind of catalyst for something – something bigger that's already happening in Batu Batur, in Sumatra, in Indonesia. I'm curious, and curiosity is winning. I'd rather be living here than dumbly dovetailing with Josh's life, Josh's ambition.

There's a distant crashing of fists on the front door. At last, some guests! But what will I do without Tengku and Umar to cook? I can't cook! And I'm still in my conservative going-to-town clothes. What if it's a good-looking bunch of Aussies, or Japanese, or better still, Brazos? What if it's Matt visiting, come to apologise, come to confess, actually Penny that wasn't my wife … Shit, what if it's Shane, back early, and his staff have disappeared? No, Shane wouldn't knock.

I lock my room, hang a left, pass four other guest bedrooms and reach the dining deck. Everything's in order. Then I head down the corridor of gut-warping surf posters, calling out 'Sorry – just a tick!'

There're five Indonesian policemen at the door. I don't recognise any of them from my police station visit after the party at Franz and Adalie's. Their faces are as hard and shiny as the backs of new shovels.

Oh fuck.

I don't play Shane's games. Don't pretend not to speak Indo.

'Selamat sore, silahkan masuk, yaaaa,' I say with faux fearlessness. Good afternoon, please come in. Please come in, and please don't notice how relieved I am for the extra length in my skirt, my sleeves.

The men follow me to the dining deck. One distinguishes himself as the officer in charge by sitting down and dumping his boots on the nearest chair. The hairs of his moustache hang over his top lip like tiny blades.

'You work here?'

'Yes, sir. Can I perhaps get you a drink, sir? We've got orange juice, Coca-Cola, tea, coffee ...'

'Yeah, I want a drink.'

He doesn't elaborate. Have I missed something critical and basic? 'Maaf ya, Pak. Mau minum apa?' Sorry sir, *what* would you like to drink?

'What else have you got?'

I rack my brains. 'Sprite, Fanta, Teh Botol ...'

Those lazy-mean eyes have infinite blinking patience.

'Lagi ada Bintang, arak, gin –'

'Whisky,' he cuts in.

He's been here before.

'Buat semua?' For everyone?

A slight inclination of the head. I hit the bar and pour generous serves, balance them back on a tray. The officer doesn't take his eyes off me as he sips. I'm tempted to get up and pour myself a whisky, or to put my feet on the chair next to the officer's; tempted to do something young and mad and indifferent, just to shatter the glassy tension. He's first to finish. He draws a single finger over his lips, asks softly, 'Dimana Shane?'

'Medan. He'll be back in two days.'

'Did he leave it?'

'Leave what?' I ask, just as it dawns on me. They're here for the bribe, of course. The bribe Shane pays to sell liquor, to stay open. Shane didn't mention they'd be coming and he certainly didn't leave any money. Perhaps they're early. 'Oh, yang itu!'

You're talking about *it*. 'I'm sorry, sir, but Shane left nothing with me to give to you. He's been very busy and actually quite sick. Perhaps if you come back on the weekend?'

'I think you can help us.'

There's something about their faces, something at once familiar and utterly strange. These police have the same look as Indonesian soldiers, or Indonesian customs officials – the ones who fleece you in small rooms, behind closed doors, over ash-stippled desks. It's a look of carefully combed contempt, backed with blankness. It's a look that makes it impossible to imagine these men as husbands, as fathers, as brothers.

'Take me to the office. You have a key to the safe.'

'I don't have a key to the safe,' I say truthfully. 'I've only been working here for a week. Shane doesn't trust me with a key to the safe.'

'Then I'm afraid, miss, you'll have to give me your passport.'

'My passport's with immigration,' I lie. 'I don't have my passport. But I'm happy to get you a photocopy.' I jump to my feet.

The officer doesn't like this. He too springs to his feet so we're eye level.

Above us, the nuts in the betel tree click like wooden beads.

'Whisky,' he says.

'Certainly, sir.'

'The bottle,' he says.

'Of course.'

I bring him an unopened bottle, our last. Hand it over with the faintest tremor in my fingers.

'You tell Shane we'll be back,' the officer says.

Then the five of them turn and head toward the door.

I can't help myself. I break into English. 'See ya later, ya fucken jerks!'

The officer turns and for a single horrified moment I worry

he's understood me. I smile and dip my head graciously. He nods. They leave. And I make straight for the remaining half-bottle of whisky.

51

Adalie texted yesterday asking me over for coffee. I'd forgotten about giving her my number at Dennis' place. Tengku and Umar had reappeared by the time I left, but Kristi was still missing. I didn't feel too bad about heading out, knowing the boys were there. I wasn't disobeying Shane's explicit demand not to leave the resort unattended.

It's hard to imagine it was only a few weeks ago I was last in this house of wood and glass, moving drunk around the laughter-lit rooms, burningly conscious of Matt. Now, it's a completely different space; the paintings are bubble-wrapped and the artifacts and textiles are bundled into boxes. The remaining glass in the window frames is held in place by brown masking tape and there's the moving-out smell of cypress-scented cleaning products.

'Come in, come in!' calls Adalie when she sees me at the door.

'Thanks. How's the packing coming along?'

'It's awful.'

'I'm sorry,' I say awkwardly.

A woman comes in from the kitchen corkscrewing a grey cleaning rag between her hands. She smiles at me, flashing neat white teeth, and asks Adalie if she has a moment.

'Tentu saja!' Of course! Adalie says in thickly Dutch-accented Indonesian.

The woman then drops to her knees in a position of

supplication and my heart drops with her – appalled.

'It's like this,' she says. 'Bu has been such a good employer over the years and I give thanks to God for bringing you to us. But I have something to ask. Yesterday, one of my sons crashed our family's only motorbike.'

Adalie is as uncomfortable as me. She's readjusting her skirt, lowering herself to the floor, taking her housekeeper's hands in her own.

Her housekeeper, almost crying, continues, 'Bu has always been so good and I'm so sorry to ask, but I wonder if you can spare some money to help fix the motorbike?'

'That is no problem,' says Adalie warmly. 'Of course I can spare you the money. How much do you need?'

Her housekeeper mumbles a rupiah equivalent of forty Australian dollars.

'Of course. No problem at all,' Adalie repeats. 'We've been so happy with the work you've done. And just because we're leaving now, it doesn't mean we won't be back, it doesn't mean we won't be in touch.'

'Thank you Bu. May you have a long life,' her housekeeper says, tears sliding freely now down her pretty, high-cheeked face.

The two women embrace. If only I'd turned up ten minutes later. This is way too intimate. The housekeeper is a proud woman – imagine the courage it must have taken for her to fold to her knees and beg. I feel slightly sick-dizzy when I think of the power of money here.

Through the glass, over the balcony, a grey wind gurneys the tops of the trees. In the distance, there's a lead-pencil line of ocean lurching with swell. So much for my plan of getting in the water.

'Sorry Penny,' says Adalie. Her housekeeper has disappeared. 'Please, come. Can I get you a coffee?'

'Sure.'

When we're finally settled in cane chairs on the balcony, sipping from glasses of grainy, tasty robusta, she says, 'Remember the meeting at Dennis'?'

I nod.

'Do you remember what Matt said?'

My cheeks spot red like stovetops. 'About what?'

If Adalie notices my shame she doesn't let on. 'About Shane. About the dukun.'

'Yeah,' I say cautiously, wondering where this is going. 'Matt was seeing a dukun to try and poison him.' While I haven't said anything to Shane, I'm carrying it, the moral baggage of complicity.

'So is it working?' Adalie's dead serious.

'I don't know. Shane's sick, there's no doubt about that.'

The wind picks up. Adalie's unruffled, face thoughtful. 'I'm about to tell you something. And I would like you to keep this just between the two of us.'

I wait.

'I've talked with my housekeeper and she's gone to see a friend. We think this will work much better. Here.' She hands me a plastic bag. Inside is a twisted black piece of ... what? Skin? Fin? Bone? Tongue?

I get a prickling feeling under my shirt that's got nothing to do with the wind. 'More black magic,' I say, surprised at how even my voice is, thinking: these mad bloody bules! First Matt, now Adalie, who else? The bules here are probably wheeling and dealing in more black magic than the locals!

'Don't say anything to Franz,' Adalie says. 'I know he's an anthropologist, but he's a scientist first. He wouldn't approve. The thing is, I really don't want to go back to Europe. Imagine – winter in Holland. Horrible! Franz says the only way we would possibly consider staying is if Shane was gone. I know, I know,' she gestures inside to the packed boxes. 'A bit late, no? But this,' she flicks the plastic bag, 'very bad, very strong. It took my housekeeper a long time to get.'

'So ... what do I –'

'Boil it. Then mix the boiled liquid in with some tea. One week within drinking it, he'll be gone. Back to Australia.'

'I don't know if Shane drinks tea. Certainly beer and spirits.'

'Well, I leave it to you.'

'Adalie, I don't mean to be disrespectful, but Shane's my boss. He's paying me, and well, he's ... well, he's not *that* bad.'

She laughs softly, mirthlessly. 'Yes, this is what you think now,' she says. 'This is what you think now.'

52

That night, after Tengku and Umar have disappeared to their room, it feels like I'm the only one in the surf resort. The wind has completely died. Waves detonate on the reef. I fidget through a few pages of Robert Adamson but feel too keyed up, too nervous to be reflective. So I toss the book and turn instead to a surf movie. There are the usual boobs and barrels and blue water. I only half watch, mind still elsewhere. I'm thinking of the police with their skin buff with sweat and oil. I'm thinking of Ibu Surti dreaming of shopping malls while Adalie dreams of magic. I'm thinking of the plastic bag with its devilish black contents scrunched out of sight in my rucksack. I'm thinking that consumerism, modernity, must be slowly eroding culture, and wonder if it will also erode religion. I'm thinking of a burning church and Josh's text in code. And suddenly, hotly, I'm thinking of Matt. Of my lips tracing his jaw, tracing a path through the raw stubble down his throat, tracing his dark, sharp collarbones. I'm thinking of his hands gliding my sides, lacing hard in the small of my back. I'm thinking: I hate being here alone. I hate sleeping alone. There's a pause in the surf movie. Beyond the guesthouse drifts the eerie electric song of the ice-cream man.

53

Kristi's back, busy airing out a bedroom. She dares me with her eyes to say something. I just smile and say good morning, head on to the kitchen to fix myself a coffee. Tengku and Umar are in their usual spot, sucking up oily strands of mie goreng.

'Hey guys, where've you been?'

'Jalan-jalan,' they reply in unison.

'But where?'

They gesture vaguely. It probably doesn't matter where they've been, it's not like we were flat out with guests.

I take my coffee onto the deck and look out over the water. It's early morning silk. The waves are lining up on the main reef okay but it's big, with the odd, rogue wash-through. Maybe I'll go for a paddle tomorrow, if the wind continues to hold off and it settles down a bit.

Around ten, Shane comes heavy-footed along the corridor of posters. He didn't look too bad the night before he left but he looks shattered now, pink-eyed and sallow-skinned. He must have driven overnight from Bandar Lampung. Still, he grins when he sees me.

'Penny! How's everything been?'

'Pretty quiet.'

'Always is this time of year. I've got some early Christmas presents for you.'

'Presents?!'

'Kristi!' he bellows.

She appears within moments, a coquettish tilt to her head.

'There's some bags on the back seat of the car. Bring them in.'

She pads away on bare feet.

'What was Medan like?' I ask.

'What do you think?'

'A shithole?'

'You got it. And so were they alright? They didn't fuck off on you?'

Maybe that's what had happened last time.

'No, no. All good.'

He can sense the lie, the way a shark senses blood. I can feel him gathering himself for an attack but Kristi comes back with the bags, distracting him.

'On the table,' he commands. 'The green one's for you.'

The bag's full of fabric – skirts, dresses, skimpy singlets.

'Thought your wardrobe needed a bit of a lift. I don't want to see you in pants anymore, especially not those fucken clown pants you had on the other night, the ones with the crotch down to the floor. They're not a good look, okay? You're working in a surf resort, not the fucken backpackers in Perth. Think of this as your uniform. And that bag too, the blue one.'

There are two bottles of Gordon's inside. I don't feel comfortable about being told what to wear, but a few bottles of bedroom gin is just fine. 'Thanks Shane.'

Kristi's pouting.

'Yeah, yeah, yeah,' he says. 'I didn't forget about you. You'll get *your* present later.'

He smacks her arse.

Somewhere in the distance, a wail from the mosque opens like a throat.

54

Shane's gesturing wildly at a bloke a third his age. There are three of them. Definitely Aussies. With sun-bleached hair and boardies and Bintang singlets that show off effortlessly toned arms. Their bare feet are a mess of reef cuts, missing toenails, inky lines of urchin poison. It looks as though Shane's trying to out-storytell the young bloke. The bloke, too stupid or arrogant to see the manic gleam in Shane's eye, keeps interrupting him. Shane doesn't flip. The night is young. The mozzie coil has only just begun its inward inch. Then one of them notices me, lets out a low, shy cough, and gestures with his head. Shane spins around.

'Penny. These gentlemen would like to order.'

'What can I get for you guys tonight?'

I take the orders for beer and then Shane turns back to the young fella. 'What were ya saying, mate?'

They only stay for a few, then take off into town in a taxi for some dinner at the night market. Shane seems disappointed to see them go and turns to me. He's got a heavy smell about him: cologne and sweat and charred cloves.

No chance, not tonight. I excuse myself and go back to my room for a quiet beer alone.

55

It's the crack of dawn and I'm up in the surf-check tower. Over the water the colours are changing, somnolent as smoke. There's one guy out surfing the right and, even from this distance, I know it's Shane. Despite his heft he's unbelievable on a board. You can tell he used to surf competitively by his wave choice, by the line he cuts, by the timing and placement of his turns. I imagined he'd surf all whack and slash, with a kind of disdain for the wave. Instead, he's got a much smoother, more powerful style. Big, relaxed turns. Big, violent fans of spray. Shane apparently doesn't just talk the talk.

Behind me, the ladder creaks and groans. The day's started. It's the three guys. Scratching their armpits and stubble.

'Morning.'

'Morning.'

'What a faggot,' one of them says. He half turns to me. 'Told us it only worked on high tide in the dry.'

This morning, it's glassy and the tide is super low. Blackened knobs of rock and reef are exposed almost to the wave. If Shane missed a take-off, he'd end up kissing dry reef. But there's no way Shane will miss a take-off.

'Looks pretty shallow,' comments another guy. 'Bet his fins are clipping the reef on those bottom turns.'

'Don't be a pussy. Let's hit it.'

A few minutes later there's the scuffing of tropical wax, the smell of coconuts and bubblegum. The guys go cat-like over the reef. Shane, when he sees them, takes a wave in.

56

A paddlepop dusk, a fluro '80s sunset: guava, violet, sirsak. The muezzin starts his dusk cry and tonight, there's something arresting in his voice, an exquisite, almost feminine mournfulness.

Shane's voice competes with the muezzin's.

'... well you know, some people like fucking blonds, others like fucking paraplegics. I happen to like fucking Asian chicks –'

The guys' laughter is punctuated with the throaty rattle of geckos.

'Penny,' says Shane when he sees me. 'Get yourself a drink and join us. Gentlemen,' he opens his hand expansively, 'can the lady sort you out with more drinks? This round's on the house.'

'We'll have three more Binnys thanks,' says one of the guys in a nasal voice. He's obviously the leader of the group, with freckles so dense they blur into a tan.

'Shane?'

He lifts his beer. 'Same again, love.'

Before sorting out the drinks at the bar I duck my head into the kitchen to make sure Tengku and Umar are on call should the guys want dinner. Kristi's sitting on an upturned crate with a cigarette resting on a sulky bottom lip. A dirty cloth hangs over her knee. A rubble of unwashed plates, spoons and ashtrays is spread across the kitchen benches. The Aussie boys must have had an early feed.

Tengku and Umar are nowhere to be seen.

'Well?' I say, gesturing to the mess.

'Well what?' she spits.

I shake my head; give up. She doesn't answer to me anyway.

At the beer fridge I pull out five frosty Bintangs. Within moments, the bottles bead with condensation. I cram them on to a tray and move back over to the guys. They scrape their chairs out to include me in the circle. Their hands – the scorched colour of crab – reach greedily for the beers.

'I was just telling the fellas what keeps me here despite all the shit. They've seen it firsthand. Tell 'er about the bikes.' Shane's already slurring his words.

'The bikes?' repeats the freckled guy. 'Yeah, well, we got in a few days ago and stayed down on the beach.'

'At Ibu Ayu's?'

'Nah, some other joint. A bloke rented us bikes for a week. On day three one of the bikes disappeared. Bang. Just like that. From the locked car park.' He caulks his beer with his lips. Wipes his mouth. Continues, 'They called up the bloke we rented them off and he demanded we cover the cost of the bike. Pay for a brand new moto.'

'Oh yeah? How much were you lookin' at?'

One of the other guys, dark skin, rum-wicked eyes, says, 'Eight grand.'

'No way! More like eight hundred,' I say. 'So what happened?'

Ants are mobilising around my beer. I lift it from the balcony railing to my lips.

The freckly guy continues. 'Obviously we were suss on the whole thing and sure enough, later that arvo, Johnno saw his bike parked out the front of the Circle K supermarket. Recognised the sticker. So we waited outside and roughed the bloke up a bit.'

Johnno, a blond surf doll, sniggers, 'Yeah, that's one way of putting it.'

Shane's not to be outdone. 'There's a syndicate of them,' he says. 'Those Euros who were here the other week, same thing happened to them.'

'They didn't rent off Ibu Ayu?'

'Course not. They were lookin' for the cheapest bikes.'

'Yeah, right.'

The conversation slides on to surfing. When I was a kid the topic always coruscated inside me: the idea of unscoured coasts, unvisited villages, the wandering promise of adventure. Then, maybe on Namotu, something hardened. I got sick of the endless speculation that went with it, like: 'You should've been here yesterday,' 'Lookin' good for Thursday, Friday,' 'On its day.'

Better to live it, not to talk it. Better to let your surfing do the talking rather than your mouth. Dad had taught me that. But surfers can go on and on for hours and not bore.

I'm bored.

My eyes quickly assess the beer situation. The boys' are still about half full. Shane's is almost empty. I slip out of my seat and back to the bar. The difference between being a waitress and a hostess. Anticipating the needs of your guests, your boss. Not waiting to be asked. I look into the kitchen again but Kristi has disappeared with the cooks. I know what will happen, I'll end up having to do the clean up later tonight, swaying on my feet from booze and weariness.

When I get back with Shane's beer, the guys have warmed up, are now dangerously squeezing him.

'So Shane, mate. How come you've named this wave out the front after yourself? When we were surfing up north this arvo and mentioned we surfed "Shane's Sumatra" this morning, the local fellas didn't have a clue what we were talking about.

They said the right-hander out the front is called Karang Kepiting.'

'Karang Kepiting?' Shane repeats. 'Never heard of it.'

'What about that set up on the way to Padang? Supposed to be like a reverse Ulus. You know how we could find it?'

'How you could find it? Get on a bike, take a map and drive.' Shane leans toward the guys, 'Once you've crossed the eighth river after the island, you're getting close. If you get to Bintuhan, you've overshot.'

In my opinion, there are two types of surfers; those who tell – who by telling feel as if they have some power over their listeners, who can't help but tell – and those who stay silent.

Shane disappoints. After a little more prodding, he explains exactly how to get there, exactly what tide to surf the reef on, exactly what wind, exactly what swell size and direction.

'It's fickle,' he warns them. 'There's a good chance you'll be skunked. If you like though, Penny can drive you there tomorrow.'

Shane pats his pocket, fumbles out a set of car keys.

'Here. The fellas will wanna leave first thing.'

'Sure.'

No doubt Matt's unimpressed when he has to share his local with guys like these. They're nice enough but young fellas' tongues run quick.

Shane seems to me a little pathetic in that moment, bulk hunched over beer, currying favour with second-hand knowledge. And then he stands, challenges one of the guys to a game of pool. The one with the flirting, rum-black eyes. 'Yeah, alright. Always keen for a bit of pool.'

Shane follows them to the table. There's the clean crack of pool balls. The guys continue their easy, piss-taking chat.

'Yeah, Rob! Sick one.'

'Didn't realise you were a pool shark, mate.'

'What's wrong with ya, Shane, beer's supposed to make you *more* focused!'

Above Shane's head, bloated bugs helicopter the lamps. He looks more than focused. His lips have thinned to a scar and there's something in his eyes, something doubling and daft. I stand quietly. Watch him line up the cue, let it rest on the bridge of his fingers, test its slide. He's three balls down. The guys fall silent, grip their beers. Shane jerks the cue. It smacks the jack. One of his balls spins toward a pocket then stops, a floss-line away.

There's an agonising silence.

Shane's fury swells the space, invisible, but palpable. And then he loses it. Snaps the pool cue against the edge of the table. Snaps it in half. The guys' mouths paralyse in sneers of disbelief.

Shane turns on them. 'What the fuck are you lookin' at, hey? *Hey*?!'

The three guys are all shorter than Shane. None of them can stare him directly in the eyes.

The blond surf doll, Johnno, puts his hands up, palms out. 'Nothin' mate. We're not lookin' at nothin'.'

But Shane isn't listening. The lines on his face are soluble as backstreet batik – in one instant distinct then rinsing soft as he moves into the light.

The guys back away, murmuring.

'Might hit the sack now, eh.'

'Not a bad idea.'

'Wanna be up early for the dawnie.'

'Yeah, for sure.'

Rob's the first to turn away, pool cue still in hand, amusement in those dark eyes. Shane pins him with a look. And then sends a loaded Bintang bottle flipping toward the back of his head. It bumps his shoulder, bursts against the floor.

'I asked *what the fuck you were looking at!*' roars Shane.

The guy touches his shoulder, turns back around, slowly.

The three of them narrow their eyes like dogs.

Rob charges, swings the cue. It connects with Shane's forehead. Shane drops to his knees. The other two guys kick him to his back. Kick him and kick him in the ribs and arse. Shane moans. For such an intimidating-looking bloke I can't believe they've toppled him so quickly.

The guys are panting, with each kick they spit, '*Fuck* you, *fuck* you, *fuck* you.'

I have to do something. But Kristi beats me to it. She's running across the deck with a bucket of water. When she's close enough, she throws it over them.

They stop, in shock. They're breathing heavily. Water trembles from their lips, their eyelashes. Then they shake themselves off.

Shane moans again.

For a moment it looks like they'll get stuck back in to him but instead, Rob delivers a quick parting kick, and then, without a glance at either Kristi or I, the three of them turn and head to their rooms.

Kristi already has Shane's head on her lap, is turning his face from side to side and inspecting the lump rising red on his forehead.

I leave him with her and start gathering the empty Bintang bottles.

*

Tossing in bed later that night I think about how quickly Shane buckled. Did it have anything to do with the dukun's spell? His temper turned so fast. After talking to the girls in the beauty salon I'd dismissed the possibility that he could have cut the fingers off that whore in Lampung. Perhaps I should have been more wary. Perhaps I should have listened to all the warnings I've had since I arrived. But you don't listen to what you don't want to hear. And I guess I have a hard time admitting when I've made a wrong decision.

57

My heart's pummelling, matching a pummelling at the door. The dark is totally disconcerting – it could be near morning or still late at night.

'Penny.' The voice is unfamiliar.

'Yeah …' I stumble toward the door, clumsily tying on my sarong, pulling my sleep-pretzeled hair into a ponytail.

I unlock the door.

'Hey Rob.'

'Hey Penny. You ready to go?'

'Give me five.'

Half an hour later I'm behind the wheel, easing the car up mountains, over landslides, around potholes. One of the potholes drops about four metres. A baby tree grows at the bottom. I can't really recall Shane's directions from the night before so I'm happy to be instructed by the guys. I caught Rob and Johnno's names last night but the third guy, the one with the freckles, is named Andy. They're all studying at uni in Adelaide but grew up on the Eyre Peninsula, an area notorious for its great whites, frigid water and heavy waves. They're not here to muck around.

'So is he always like that?' Johnno's in the passenger seat and his eyes take a pale, Vaseline slide from my face to chest.

'I don't know, I haven't been working for him for long.'

'What a hectic cunt,' says Andy.

'Yeah.' Last night scared the hell out of me. And somehow,

I don't think Shane's temper was even properly articulated. He capitulated too quick.

Rob echoes my thoughts, 'I would've thought for a bloke his size, he would've had a bit more fight in him.'

I don't answer.

'Hey Pen, hang a left here. Let's check this track,' says Johnno. We cut through rice paddies toward the coast, end up on an empty black-sand beach watching glassy four-foot peaks. 'This is us!'

'Looks good, but it isn't the reverse Ulus we've heard about. I'm keen for some reef,' says Andy. 'What d'you reckon, Rob?'

'Whatever. Probably rather surf a reef.'

So it's back in the car.

I'd forgotten about this. The maddening search. The way you can drive for an hour, check ten different spots, and end up back where you started. But today, I don't let it bother me. I'm glad for an excuse to be away from Shane's.

We check another few spots and then end up passing through a small fishing village. Smoke hangs above the bougainvillea and the wooden rooftops and there are trays of tiny fish drying in the sun. We stop at the village market for a quick snack then head on, mouths flushed with instant coffee and sharp with the tang of star fruit. The road peters out in a car park overlooking a bay.

'Fuck yeah!' says Andy.

It's still no reverse Uluwatu but there's a wave and it's barrelling and it's underscored with reef. The setup is unusual: a giant fist of rock is separated from the mainland by a twenty-five metre passage of water. The swell seems to be both pushing through the passage and around the rock, wedging in a heavy, fast right. We watch a few come through and it looks manageable. I might have had a crack, straight off the back of Fiji. Then a wave explodes over the rock and we all inhale sharply. A wedge jacks up, three times as big as any before it.

'It's just like Tchopes!' Johnno jokes, even though the only similarity with Tahiti's Teahupoo might be the thrill and terror of surfing it big. The other two snigger but don't take their eyes off the wave; we're all wondering if the reef will hold the size.

A perfect cylinder opens, big enough to park a garbage truck, or drop a donga in. We watch it curtain, reel down the line, and then spit, a powerful discharge of air and spray. The water seethes.

'What the fuck's that?' Rob's pointing.

'What the fuck's what?' Andy's squinting.

'There's guys up there on the cliff, fishing. See?'

'Yeah. So?'

'They've got their lines smack bang on the take-off. Look!'

He's right, there's a row of men crouched on the cliff above the wave; there's the diagonal gleam of fishing lines.

'Oh well. Guess we'll just have to dodge 'em!' Rob peels off his shirt.

Oh shit, I think, too nervous to appreciate the dark ripple of his abs. What if one of the guys ends up with his face rearranged on the reef, or with a fishing hook jammed through the back of his thigh?

'Let's hit it, then,' says Johnno.

Without planning to, they time their paddle perfectly and end up out the back with dry hair at a rough approximation of the take-off point. The fishermen watch them. They watch the horizon. Behind us in the village, a local mosque crackles to life. Those shivery, keening Arabic vowels lift and seem to catch in the sea mist.

And nothing happens.

It's as if the ocean has taken a long inward breath.

After a bit, I grab my sarong from the car, halve it, and lay it flat next to a tree. Next time I'll bring a camera. If I had a good camera and took proper shots I could sell them. That's what the kids do at Ulus, that's what we did on Namotu. And it would be great to get some photos for the new website. But would there be a next time? If Shane threw a bottle at my head, there'd be no way Kristi would be running to the rescue with an icy bucket of water. Maybe the money isn't worth it. Maybe it is time to cut and run. I've got enough to stay in Indo for a couple of months without working. I should go and talk to Dennis about it, maybe after I drop the guys off. They've got all their gear with them, so they're probably planning on heading back to Batu Batur to find a new place to stay.

Out in the surf they're getting impatient, bored. Rob disappears underwater, probably to check the depth. Johnno paddles closer to shore and waits for a smaller one. Hold your ground! I want to shout at him. It's Indo, it's long period, you'll get got! But I hold my tongue. He's too far out to hear me anyway. When a wave finally wraps around the rock, the first in a set of eight, they're nowhere near where they should be for the take-off. Eight unridden barrels, from head-high to overhead, churn green and spit white.

And then the ocean starts to breathe.

Set after set curves around the rock and into the bay.

Although the first few are head-high, the take-off is still critical – a vertical drop, a quick race, a hand in as the curtain closes. Johnno and Andy are on their forehand, which means they're facing the wave, but Rob is struggling on his backhand. On his first wave, he's too slow taking off and the wave's lip clips the back of his head and sends him flying, smacks him under. For a few horrifying moments his board tombstones white, then falls flat and he's up.

Another few sets and they're starting to read it, knowing

exactly when to jump, pump, stall. They move deeper and now they're dangerously close to the fishermen's lines. In fact, Andy could just about reach out and touch one.

The next set is big and the third wave in the set is a bomb that cracks over the rock and swallows it entirely. Andy's paddling for the horizon. A wedge grows: black, steep, and bigger than anything that's come through this morning. The lip on it would snap a board clean. There's no way Andy's gunna make it over. He's gunna cop this monster on the head. The top of the wave feathers. He starts to paddle up the face of it. Then abruptly, he swings his board. He's going for it! He drops, vertical, and almost comes unstuck before the board finally connects with water. And then he's enveloped. It's not a perfect Indo barrel – far from it. It's warped and rogue and gets bigger as it runs down the line. Andy's inside for ten thrilling seconds then is spat out screaming high-pitched bliss.

That's when the fishermen crack.

They've been composed up until this point, almost statuesque, patiently absorbed in the pursuit of pelagics, saturated in mid-morning sun. Now they're on their feet, yelling, shaking their fists and drawing in their lines. They must think the guys scared away the fish.

Rob and Johnno don't seem to notice. A small wave pushes through, but neither of them want it. They want a wave like Andy's. They want a bomb.

The fishermen are moving in single file, marching down the ridgeline toward the beach. Andy's seen them and he's paddling for shore. I run to the edge of the water, shouting to attract Rob and Johnno's attention, but they don't see me, don't hear me, they're too far out. Andy puts his fingers in his mouth, loosing a shrill whistle. That gets their attention. He points at the fishermen. Rob and Johnno look lazily, but do nothing. It seems as if they'll keep surfing. The fishermen are almost at the bottom of the cliff. They're minutes away at most.

Just as I'm wondering whether Andy and I should jump into the car and leave them, Rob and then Johnno pick off small ones, race along the face, dive onto their bellies and glide the whitewater to shore. By the time they reach the car, I've got the engine running, the handbrake off and my foot quivering above the accelerator. There's no time to strap the boards on the roof – they get thrust in the boot, spearing over the back seat so Andy and Rob have to fold around them. Johnno's barely piled into the front seat when my foot falls and the car leaps forward.

'Go Penny. Go, go, go!'

There's a sound, like spit.

The back windscreen ripples, then folds.

We're chased out by a blizzard of threats and rocks.

It's late afternoon by the time we get to Batu Batur. I drop the guys at Ibu Ayu's. Ibu's not around but Cahyati comes to the gate, smiling. I help the guys unpack and turn down Rob's offer for afternoon beers, pretending not to notice his lingering eyes. They tell me they haven't fixed up anyone for their rooms and are tempted not to pay at all, except that'd mean Shane would serve me shit when I got back, and they don't want that. So they give me money for the rooms, the car hire and a bit toward the back windscreen. None of us have any idea what that might come to.

'Guess I'll see ya at Shane's again next year!' I call out the window as I reverse.

They crack quick grins then become serious again, contemplating the wax on their surfboards. It's studded with white diamonds of windscreen glass.

58

As I pass the Circle K on my way out of town, I double-take. A man out the front lifts his hand. I almost veer into the path of a sand-loaded truck, nerves sparking. It's Josh. Perth Josh. Boyfriend Josh. Josh is here. The truck blasts me. I pull over. Swing a U-turn. He looks totally out of place, red-cheeked and perspiring.

'Pen,' his voice, soft and loyal, lifts shingles of guilt along my neck.

'Josh. What the fuck. What are you doing here?'

The whole thing seems completely surreal. To be pulled up outside the Circle K in Batu Batur with Josh standing there, my eyes full of truck grit, heart full of remonstration.

'There's something I want to tell you.'

'To tell me?'

He doesn't move forward. He doesn't try to touch me.

I manage to stumble through the words, 'Well, should we go for a coffee then?' They sound stiff and awkward and formal.

'Yeah,' he says. 'Let's do coffee.'

'Do coffee,' I think as he slides into the passenger seat. '*Do coffee.*' Like I'm a fucking client. We drive in silence. At least if we were on a motorbike there might be some kind of forced intimacy. His chest warm along my back. A hand on my thigh. But then, I don't know how I'd deal with this. And what is it he wants to tell me? Maybe he wants to tell me to come home with him.

I start constructing the scenario in my head … not yet, I need independence, space. Actually, I have a lover. Actually, maybe we should be over. I'm flattered, I'll say, I'm flattered you've come all this way for me. And I'll mean it. And I'm terrified how he'll react when I disappoint him. Then again, maybe he's not going to tell me to come home with him, maybe he's over for Christmas instead. It'll be Christmas next week.

Up at Roger's, everything's sharp, the bamboo and frangipanis are cut with cartographic precision.

We talk small. Josh asks if I've settled in, how it's going.

I give him a sanguine, if somewhat untruthful, picture of my time here. Don't mention the panic and adrenaline of the morning. Or last night. Or the police visit …

Our coffees arrive.

Josh looks at his hands. 'I don't quite know how to say this, Penny,' he begins.

He looks different. His hair is longer, there's more grey in it. His shoulders are bigger, and it looks like he's not just running but that he might be swimming again and back on the weights. He's calm and grave as usual but there's something else in his countenance, the throb of some unknown impulse, new to me. New and almost exciting.

'This is really hard for me,' he says, and spontaneously, sympathetically, I reach out and take his hand.

He gently wrings it free.

'I, um. I've been seeing someone,' he says.

My coffee mug is almost to my lips. I stare at him over the rim in disbelief. 'What?'

'Well, not just "someone". I'm actually back with the ex.'

The cup slides, coffee spills, my fingers burn.

'Oh.' That's all I can manage. I draw out a serviette, start wiping.

'Penny? Come on, Pen, at least look at me. At least say something.'

I stop wiping.

'Pen?'

'You came all this way to tell me *that*?'

'Well, yes and no. Jessica and I are having Christmas in Bali.' He seems relieved to be able to explain himself. 'Our flights were via Jakarta so I thought the right thing to do would be to tell you in person. I flew to Bandar Lampung then got a driver from the airport but we didn't get in until late last night. I was going to drop by Shane's tomorrow morning to see you, then head back to Bandar Lampung tonight. But there you were.'

'But here I am.'

He's still looking at me, evenly, honestly. 'I also wanted to bring you the rest of your things. You didn't leave much but … well, Jessica's moved back in.'

All that indecision. All that guilt. For what?

'Okay,' I say.

'Okay? Is that all?'

'No. That's not all. Can you leave my things at Ibu Ayu's?'

'Sure. That's actually where I stayed last night.'

I manage to lift my eyes to his. I wish with that look he could know my question, wish he could feel the terrible deadness and storm in my heart. 'What happened?'

'It probably started six months ago. We ran into each other in town, went for a coffee. Probably a month before you left we were sleeping together –'

'No, I don't care about that. I mean what happened with me? What was it about me?'

First Matt, now Josh. Or really, first Josh, then Matt.

'Nothing,' he says. He's lying, trying to soften it.

'Tell me.'

'Look, how do I say this? I was reading something on the plane, in the inflight magazine. In the article the journo reckoned you learn more about a man through his plans than any other way. Because plans are daydreaming and that's the absolute measure of a man.'

'Well, I'm not a man,' I say hotly, childishly.

He ignores me. 'But I never know what you've planned, you're always drifting, you're never quite present. Always watching but never quite involved. You've got no goals, no drive. How can I try to structure my own life around you, when you can't even tell me what you're doing? Where you're going? When you'll be home?' Then, with the faintest hint of accusation, 'Were you even planning on coming back?'

My fingers grope against the wooden table in search of the car keys. The waitress is approaching the table with our lunches. I can't stay a moment longer.

'It doesn't matter,' I say, eyes wet. 'None of it matters.'

'I'm sorry, Penny,' he says. 'I'm so, so sorry.'

I get out of there before I start bawling.

59

The machete swing of a setting sun: within moments it'll bury itself in the water. There's a bule in the surf-check tower, long-limbed, his rapt, soft-eyed gaze spelled by the wave.

When Shane storms out onto the balcony in a Bintang singlet fingered by years of laundering in unfiltered tap water, his bruised face spasms.

'Oi!'

The belting has clearly done nothing to curb Shane's aggression. If anything, he seems worse.

The bloke in the tower turns around.

'What the fuck do you think you're doing up there?'

'Just checking –'

'Just *nothing*,' Shane barks. 'That view's for paying customers only.'

The bloke thinks it's a joke, his lips twitch to smile. But when he sees the look on Shane's face, he quickly climbs down.

'Whaddyawant?'

'Someone in town told me you do board repairs.' He's Irish.

'Yeah? Well I don't. Anything else?'

'No, no, I suppose that was it.' The bloke has pale eyes, is sunburnt to the wrists. He isn't fixing for a fight.

I find myself looking on with indifference. All my nerve endings are dead. My capacity for empathy exhausted. Maybe I should be scared, should get the hell away from this deadly lime-lick of coast, but for the moment, I feel only a crushing apathy. I sit down. Apparently I have no imagination, no plans. It probably serves me right; I asked for him to explain.

I slide my feet from my thongs. The Irishman casts me a curious look as he leaves.

Shane turns on me. 'What do you think you're doing sitting down? Sort a man out with a drink, will ya.'

I slide my feet back into my thongs.

When I join Shane with beers it doesn't seem like a good idea to bring up the windscreen.

He looks dreadful. Battered blood vessels hook against a yellowing cheek. There's a cut on his forehead, the crinkled ball-bag sag of his throat.

'What's up with you?' he says. 'No-one likes a sulky woman. Did those pricks leave money for their rooms and the car hire?'

I nod.

'Good.'

Around us, the rip and slither of a tropical night. If I keep sulking he might snap again so I rouse myself, ask something that's been at the back of my mind for weeks. 'Is there much malaria here?'

Shane takes out a packet of cigarette papers, a tin of tobacco.

'Reckon I got a dose of it right now.' He taps out a line of tobacco.

'Oh yeah, what does it feel like?'

'Like shit.' Shane rolls his cigarette with a massive hand.

Suddenly there's a hatch of moths. It starts with five, then they multiply; there are ten, there are hundreds, grilling themselves against halogen, beating tough, translucent wings. We watch the carnage in silence.

At last I ask, 'Shane, what were you doing up in Aceh?'

And that does it. That softens him. Because he's lonely.

Because he's past his prime. Because no-one is interested in his stories anymore.

'Why?' he asks gruffly, but I can tell it's a front.

'I was just wondering. I'm keen to hear about the waves.'

'Love,' he says, 'you shoulda been there thirty years ago.'

I bite back a grin. Sip my beer. Feel it chill my lips then burn as it streaks into my stomach. I plan on putting a few of these away tonight.

'The only bules there were a coupla French dickheads who'd married locals and ran some basic accom,' Shane's saying. 'That was it. Not like now. Aceh'll be the next big thing. You just wait, in ten years that place'll be crawling with Swedes and Germans who've come to Indo to "do the surfing"'. He scoffs and a tiny orb of spit catches in his stubble. 'When I first got there, I walked the coastline from Lhok Nga to Tapaktuan, looking for waves.'

'Jeez! Were you alone?'

'Course I was alone. Not many people got the guts to do something like that.'

He's right. At home, most people won't surf a wave they can't park in front of.

'When I found surf, I pitched my tent and stayed until the swell died.'

'Did anyone hassle you? For camping, I mean?'

'Wasn't the people I was worried about.'

'No?'

'Nah.'

He can tell my interest is piqued so he takes the opportunity to stand, stretch his oiled muscles. Kristi must have given him a massage this afternoon. 'Gotta piss.'

I'm convinced half of what he'll say tonight will be bullshit, the other half disfigured by time and memory. When he comes back, he tells me about a fishing village he stayed at along the way. The village was built into the side of a hill, a series of terraces stepping down to the ocean with an escarpment soaring above. Ladders and crooked staircases connected people's gardens and rice plots to their homes.

'There was no electricity. Not back then. At night, if you were on the beach looking back up, the lamps looked like strings of fairy lights.' Shane stubs out his rolly. 'I set up my tent but a local family insisted I stay with them, so I did. Every month they had a market on the soccer field, and I happened to be there for it.'

Shane's voice is changing. Bravado coalesces with nostalgia.

'This market wasn't your ordinary Thursday market or night market. The people from the mountains would come down and trade with the people from the sea. So, you know, strawberries in exchange for fish. And when I say come down I don't mean hop on a bus. It'd take 'em four days walk to get there, through the jungles and over the rivers. All day they'd trade fish. All night they'd trade women.'

He's there. Reliving the buttery exhalations of kerosene lamps, the flash of red in a kain sarong, the perfect symmetry of a village girl's face.

'I never wanted to leave. It was the most beautiful place I have ever been.'

'So why did you?'

A breeze stirs around our ankles, lifts the burnt wings of the moths.

'I fell in love.'

'Oh yeah.'

'With a girl from the mountains. Ended up walking back to her village and then got blackmailed by her dad into fighting for GAM.'

'*What?!*' He's talking about the Free Aceh Movement.

'Yep.'

Shane stands, whips off his singlet.

Tattooed in a rainbow across his chest are the words, 'Merdeka atau Mati.' Freedom or Death.

'Holy shit.'

He slings his singlet over the back of the chair, sits down again. His leathery stomach sags over the waistband of his boardies.

My mind's moving fast. What did he see? How long did he fight with them? What happened to the girl? Did he kill anyone? How did he get out of there? I think again of the dukun, of the spell, of my promise to tell him. The questions will have to wait. 'Shane, sorry to change the subject,' I rush, 'but I just remembered, I've been wanting to tell you this for a few days, I … I think you're being black-magicked.'

'What? Where the hell did that come from?'

'Just from … well, it was just something I heard and I've been meaning to tell you because I thought you should know.' I run my words together nervously. Don't mention the twisted black thing Adalie gave me.

Shane's eyes turn mean. 'Who?'

'What?'

'Who's doing it? Who's putting black magic on me?'

'I dunno.'

He leans forward so his face is a foot from my face. I'm terrified. Not sure whether he's about to bite me or kiss me. But I don't show it. Like with dogs. I move my face an inch closer to his.

'I said, I don't know.'

He growls in the back of his throat. Leans back. 'I don't give a shit. Doesn't work on bules anyway. I just want to sit here, drink my beer, and be left the fuck alone. And if any of those cunts get in the way, I'll give 'em a kick that'll send 'em back up the trees.'

60

Breathing yeast into my coffee this morning, my mind finally turns to Josh. I managed to keep it out of my mind last night. But now, with the pounding despair of a tropical hangover, I think about the situation. I don't have a place to live in Perth anymore. Don't have to worry about keeping Josh hanging. Don't have to feel guilty about sleeping with Matt, the handsome prick, though I still feel terrible for Matt's wife. But most critically, I don't have to stay at Shane's just to prove something to Josh, to prove I have direction or goals or vision or drive or commitment or whatever. I wanted the space. And this is what it looks like.

On the ride out to Dennis' during my afternoon break I'm gripped with a familiar sensation. The hangover shifts and just for a few moments I'm filled with an expansive irrational wonder, coupled with that wild sadness that comes with the consciousness of temporality. The plants seem as if they're being steamed on their stems, the mountain line is glossy as crushed charcoal, the palms spin gold light like windmills. It's so, *so* beautiful and I gorge, the way a poet might; to absorb, to distil, so I will remember, heart stuffed up thick and sad in my throat, tiny bugs from the rice fields gluing and drowning in the corners of my eyes.

There's no way Josh could ever compete with my need for this place.

And then the hangover returns.

61

A few kilometres from the turn-off to Dennis' village I see the Kiwi flying past in the opposite direction. I slow, look over my shoulder. She's pulled over. I turn around, skid to a halt next to her.

'Penny!'

'Marika, how are ya?'

'I just wanted to say goodbye.'

'Goodbye? Where are you off to?'

She's dressed as conservatively as she was at Dennis' barbecue.

'I'm not off anywhere. But I reckon you might be. Has your boyfriend come to take you home?' she smirks.

I almost burst into tears but I catch myself, say evenly, 'No, he hasn't come to take me home.' I shift the bike to neutral. 'What's up with the clothes? You goin' somewhere special?'

'Actually, I can't wear singlets at the moment.'

'What do you mean?'

'I had an accident.'

'An accident? What, on the moto?'

Two little kids wobble past on a bicycle, both balancing on the seat.

'No, in the surf.' Her flawless hot-pink manicure claws the throttle. 'I was surfing Larry's Left.'

Matt had mentioned Larry's Left. It's one of the heaviest waves in the area, mostly surfed by bodyboarders looking for cement-thick pits. A few surfers give it a crack from time to time but the general consensus is that the take-off is not worth the barrel. If the Kiwi surfs that, then she must be good. Like, *really* good.

'And …?'

She's struggling to find the words.

'And I scraped my tits off.'

An involuntary hand goes to my chest. 'You *what*?!'

'I didn't take off deep enough. If you don't want to get caught up in the lip then you almost have to backdoor it.'

'Right.'

'And I fucked it. It's so shallow out there.'

'Holy shit. So, what happened? Did you get dragged across the reef?'

'Yep …'

'And so, did you like, just scrape up your boobs or did your nipples come off?' How did that work? Do nipples even grow back?

'Nah, just my boobs. They've scabbed up okay. But you know what it's like here, trying to keep stuff from getting infected. It's so hard.' Tears carve up her blush.

Dad used to take to my coral cuts with relish. He scrubbed them out with an old toothbrush, dug around with the tweezers, then sealed them off with Obat Cina.

But *boobs*. Bloody hell. That's a bit different to a few scratches on your feet.

'When did you do it?'

The Kiwi kills the ignition of her bike.

'Few days before that barbecue at Dennis'.'

'I've still got a few antibiotics from Aus if you want them?'

'I'll be okay. Picked up some over-the-counter stuff.' She grins through tears.

'You don't think it's a good idea to head home until it heals?'

'I can't really go home because of a scratch. You know, with the business.'

I find myself wondering what will happen to her. If she'll last here in Batu Batur or if there's something that will eventually break her.

'So if you're not leaving soon then I guess I'll see you around,' she says, flicking over the ignition. Her bike starts with a roar.

'Yeah about that ... it's not going too good at Shane's. I actually think he's pretty dangerous.'

'Took you long enough to figure that one out.'

'The other night, he lobbed a Bintang bottle at one of the guests. And with Matt and Joni putting black magic on him ... I don't know him well enough to say if it's working, but anyway. Maybe if I'm still around next week we should catch up for a drink? What are you doing for Christmas? You're obviously not heading home?'

'I'm having Chrissy here. What day is it again?'

'Next Saturday.'

'Yeah cool. I think Dennis and Meri were talking about having something at their place.'

'I'm actually on my way there now,' I say.

'Nice. Tell 'em I said hi.' She looks ahead at the road for a moment. Her board is strapped to racks on the side of her bike. She must be angling for a dusk session, hoping for a glass-off. Kind of crazy, with a wound like that. No wonder she's struggling to stave off infection! She doesn't look at me when she says, 'He's not your boyfriend anymore, is he?'

'Nah.' How does she know? Maybe she was the one who drove him home from Roger's. Maybe he dropped in to her internet cafe to get in touch with the ex. It doesn't really matter.

'Are you okay?' she asks, still looking down the road.

'It could've been worse.'

I could've still been in Perth; could've just got kicked out of his apartment with all my stuff, could've had no other love interest to divert my attention, even if that, too, turned out badly.

'Cool, take it easy then,' she says.

'Sure.'

62

I circle the village twice before remembering which is Dennis and Meri's house. Distances are different on a bike and I'm coming from the opposite direction to town. The door is open and I call out.

'Sebentar!' comes Meri's reply.

She greets me a moment later, tasting spoon in hand.

'I'm just cooking something, come in, come in.' I follow her through to the kitchen and she returns to her pot. She's stirring a tofu curry. It's full of dry, floating chillies. On the chopping board next to her pot is a bunch of leaves, some kind of fragrant herb.

'What's that, Bu?'

'Kemangi. Try some.' She passes me a leaf.

Some of the herbs and vegetables here can be evilly bitter, like whatever was cooking in the dukun's shack, but this tastes like basil with a twist of lemon.

'That's amazing. I've never seen this at any of the warungs around here.'

'Yes, not so much of it here. It's Dennis' favourite. He tried it for the first time when we were in West Java and then brought some seeds back. We have a little patch –' she points through the window.

'Cool. Where is Dennis? I wanted to have a chat to him.'

'He should be on his way home from work now. He won't be long.'

'Is it okay if I wait around?'

'Of course! There're some books and magazines in the lounge room. Can I get you something to drink? Iced tea, coffee, water?'

Dennis has a fabulous collection of books in Indonesian and English. And poetry; there is a whole shelf dedicated to Australian poetry. I domino, one by one, volumes by John Tranter, Alan Wearne, Dorothy Porter, Rebecca Edwards, Bruce Beaver, Dorothy Hewett, Merlinda Bobis, Gig Ryan, John Forbes. What a goldmine! A battered cover open on the chair catches my eye: *Poetry Australia, 1975*. I turn the fan on high and start to flip the pages. Ibu moves around the kitchen and chooks cluck and kick in the yard. After a few minutes I find a poem that rivets me, makes me oblivious to everything else, takes me to Papua New Guinea with a missionary in 1891:

> ... And always outside his mosquito net
> A thousand small shrill voices sing and drone.
> Those circling deaths with wings soft as starlight ...
> ... And one day a soft breeze will fan his neck,
> And gently settle there and itch and kill ...

My scalp prickles, as if doused in cold water. Why can't they just let the malaria get him? What could possibly be worse?

'Hi Penny, I see you've found Mr Lehmann.'

I jerk my head around.

'I'm sorry, I didn't mean to startle you. You haven't been here long?'

I pull myself together. 'No, no, I ... wow.' I stand and shake his hand.

Dennis is dressed in long pants and a sensational batik shirt. When I ask where he got it he tells me he personally selected the material in Yogyakarta then took it to one of the city's best tailors. Impressive as his outfit is, he looks like he's stinking hot.

'I've been in the classroom all morning overseeing some construction. I'll just have a rinse then join you.'

'No worries.'

I go back to the poem. The poet's grandfather, a missionary, is dying. He built his church in a 'country brooding like a dark green brain', and now boards a ship home to Sydney. Coming through the Heads, 'Wind and white sails, sunlight and the salt sting.' When he arrives home his children don't recognise him. 'Strangeness hangs around him like a wind.'

I take a breath and gently close the book. But it lingers.

'That's much better.' Dennis has changed into a sarong and a singlet. Meri is behind him carrying a tray with two glasses of iced tea.

'I wish I'd noticed these earlier. I would've come over and asked to borrow some.'

It's as if Dennis is following my train of thought. 'So do you like working for Shane?'

'Well ...' I leave it there.

'That bad?'

'It's pretty bad.'

'I'm glad you dropped by. I was planning on coming to see you myself this afternoon.'

Behind us the fan blade slows, stops. The electricity has dropped out.

Dennis continues, 'You see, there's a few things you've gotta understand about what it's like to live in a community like this. Firstly, no-one respects the police. So often when there's something to be resolved, the community take it into their own hands. And it can be brutal. Years ago, when Meri and I first moved here, we had some money and jewellery stolen from our house. We talked about it with our neighbours and found out they were being robbed as well. This went on for a few months until at last someone caught the thief. He was a young man from Padang who'd been living here for six months.'

Dennis' hands, folded in his lap, are like sea-creatures that have been left out on the sand. Dried up and peppered with sunspots. He's looking at the floor.

'I was on my way to work one morning when I noticed a group of men at the edge of the rice paddy. I slowed. There was someone on the ground. A young man with his feet and hands trussed up like a pig's. He had no shirt on and all over his chest –' Dennis slashes his singlet with a finger. 'They'd cut him up with their machetes. And they were dragging him away from the road and into the rice field.'

He presses his glasses up the bridge of his nose. And finally looks at me.

'Well, nothing went missing after that. But I didn't stop, Penny. I knew it was wrong, and I didn't stop to help the man.'

I take a sip of my tea, crunch pearls of ice.

'It's the only time I saw something like that with my own eyes. Meri tells me it's not uncommon. Usually, if someone acts out against the community, they get taken fishing.'

'Uh-huh.' I can see where he's going with this. The other night, before Rick had cut him off, he told a story in a similar way. Connecting events, connecting similarities, trying to show us that there's always cause and effect and that it's always bigger than one person, one incident, especially here.

'So, are you saying the blokes have something like this in store for Shane?'

'No. I think they have something much, much worse in store for Shane. If what Meri heard at the markets this morning is anything to go by, then I must warn you, urgently, to leave. Leave Shane's as soon as you can. There's a bus out of here tomorrow morning at five. Get on that bus. Because you've been working there, you've been affiliated with him. They won't spare you.'

My throat narrows, my toes start to dance.

'Who are they? Who's planning something against him? Is it the "radicals"?' I invert my fingers around the word, conscious of Dennis' reluctance to brand, to tag, to play into the spin.

'I can't say for sure, but I think the discontent is bigger than a few hardline Islamists. I think the whole community wants Shane gone.'

'Right.'

The fan stutters alive again. We look at each other.

'But –' I'm about to sound mercenary, 'Shane owes me some money. Not a lot of money, just a bit. Should I ask for it tonight? Or do you think he'll get suspicious? Think I might be planning to bail?'

'What exactly did he promise you?'

I explain the deal, tell him about the bonus.

He's too polite to laugh. Instead, he says, 'Did you ever hear anything about that girl who was working for him? She was also promised a bonus – I think she was with him for a year or more. He refused to pay her. Probably had no intention of paying her to begin with. You never signed any contract?'

I shake my head.

'It wouldn't matter anyway,' Dennis says, 'he could have easily typed something up on a Word document. Well, as it turned out, Yuliana was a spirited young lady. And she had every intention of taking what Shane owed her. So she did. And then she left – she was from Bandar Lampung originally. Shane's careful never to employ locals. That orang lain thing. If he'd been employing people from Batu Batur he would've been kicked out years ago.'

'And Yuliana?' I ask, afraid to hear.

'Shane really had it in for Yuliana. He followed her. Found her. Then cut off her fingers for stealing. So what are you waiting for?' he says. 'Fuck the money, girl. Get back there and pack your bags.'

63

There's a police truck in the car park. While I'm tempted to come back in an hour or so when the police will surely be gone, I'm more tempted by the prospect of packing. Dennis has made the danger, the urgency, seem real and immediate. If Dennis reckons it's time to go – patient, calm, IT-nerd Dennis – then it's time to go.

The police are on the dining deck with Shane, and I try to sneak past, courting the shadows along the far wall. Shane spots me.

'Penny!'

There's a reptilian stillness about the police and a ticking, twitching, percussive paranoia about Shane.

'They say they came through the week.'

'They did. You were in Medan.'

'Well why the fuck didn't you say something?'

'I expected they'd come back. They come every month, don't they?'

'What did you give 'em?'

'Bottle of whisky. And glasses of whisky while they were here.'

'Alright.' He looks at me evenly. His look says, Penny, it's us and them.

'Now listen to me, bencong.' Shane steps up close to the police officer.

The officer is not sitting down tonight.

'I'm not happy with the pressure you put on my staff while

I was away. I'm sure we've spoken about this before. You want your money? Well, it's all yours.'

Shane reaches into his pocket and pulls out a slab of rupiah fastened with an elastic band. He slides off the elastic band and starts to flip the notes from the wad onto the wooden deck. He's flipping two thousands, five thousands, ten thousands, twenty thousands, green notes, purple notes, rust-coloured notes, Monopoly-coloured notes; but worse, he's disrespecting the higher denominations, he's flipping fifty thousands, one hundred thousands: nothing to us, everything to them.

'You want your money?' says Shane. 'Here's your money, mate. You want it that fucken bad, then you can bend down and pick it up.'

The officer's motionless. His eyes, level with Shane's armpit, are flat and motionless.

A fan whisks the air above us.

There's the rasp of rupiah on wood.

'Ambil itu,' says the police officer.

His men drop to their knees and sweep up the money, quick as they can.

When they're standing again, the police officer steps closer to Shane. 'I kill you,' he says calmly.

'Yeah, good luck with that, mate. You'll have to beat the fucken mosquitoes to it. Righto. Chop chop. Fuck off now, you've got your cash. No whisky. Tidak ada whisky. Sudah diminum by you, bencong!' Shane swings his arm in the direction of the door.

'I kill you,' the police officer repeats. 'Malam ini, I kill you.'

And this time, he trims it with a wicked smile.

64

My bags are packed and ready. I'm just going to boost. Early. Pre-dawnie. Leave a note. I'll head to Ibu Ayu's first, drop back the motorbike, pick up my things. I didn't leave much in Josh's apartment. Some books, clothes, perfumes, photos. It probably all fits in a single box. Ibu Ayu should be able to tee me up a lift with her driver. If not, then the morning bus at five. Then Lampung, then Bali. Then what? Then whatever.

It is as if the night has been gagged. Instead of chooks, geckos, coughs, growls, motorbikes that won't start, the tick-tick-tick of a fan, water flushing – there's nothing. Just the pale humid calm before rain.

*

At first I think it's the mosquitoes that have woken me. Despite the net, bites sequin my belly and I've drawn blood in my sleep, scratching. Then I hear thumping. I slide out of bed and pull on jeans and a t-shirt. The key jams in the door lock and it takes a moment for it to open. More thumping and sobs. It sounds like Shane's belting Kristi. I go quietly along the balcony, the wooden boards cool under my feet. There are no lights on, there's no moon, or phosphorescent water, or fireflies, just the sweating shadows of wood.

Turning the corner, I almost trip over a dark parcel on the ground, all nude folded legs and mussed hair. It's Kristi.

'Kristi. Hey Kristi. Kamu oke?'

There's a glistening arc of moisture curving from her lower lip to chin. Her hands bunch at her crotch and her eyelids are gummed shut with blood.

'Where's Shane?' I snarl.

'Penny, bukan Shane. Bukan Shane.' It wasn't Shane.

'Jadi siapa?'

'Six of them.'

'Six of siapa?'

She just shakes her head.

'Oh fuck.'

The thumping continues.

'Come on then.' My voice cracks with fear. 'Come back to my room. I'll give you the key. You can lock yourself in. I'll stay with you if you like.'

She shakes her head vehemently. 'They tell me, no moving. If I move … very very bad.'

Thumpthumpthump. My heart's quickening to match it.

'Come on Kristi, you'll be safe with me. You're not safe here.'

My fear's splintering into hysteria.

'No,' she says, firmly and finally.

I'm torn. I don't want to leave her, but feel sick with the thought of the six men and what they might do to me, feel sick with the memory of Dennis' warning.

'Okay, look. I've gotta get some stuff. But I'll be back in less than a minute.'

She doesn't answer.

I sprint to my room, grab the shoulder bag packed with my motorbike key, my passport, my money and cards. Then I race back out to where I left Kristi, but she's gone. In her place, there are a dozen coin-sized smudges of blood. Where did she go? Was she dragged over the balcony? Did she pick herself up and run? Do I get out of here, or do I go and find her?

The thumping gets louder. It's coming from the front door. Maybe Kristi went there, in search of Shane. I'll have a quick look and if there's no Kristi, then I'm out of here. At the end of the corridor, at the front door, there's a lump against the wall, an area of concentrated darkness. At first I think it's Kristi, but as my eyes adjust I see that it's Shane and that he's holding a gun. He swings it at me and, against the shadows, I can make out the two blown fuses of his eyes.

'Shut ya face,' he hisses, even though I haven't said a word, then to the door, loud and manic, 'Open the door! Bukalah pintu ini, you fucken anjing! You dogs!'

'What's goin' on?'

'They've nailed shut the fucken door.'

I'm already moving, I'm talking fast and frightened. 'Well what about the verandah? The track down to the beach? Come on, Shane, let's get out of here!'

There's no-one on the verandah but I hear soft voices somewhere beneath my feet. I creep to the handrail by the stairs, peer through the leaves. The track down to the beach seems clear. Maybe I misplaced the voices, maybe they've been misshaped by night, maybe they're actually coming from the front door. Shane hasn't followed.

There's an eruption of bats. A shout from below.

I forget about Shane. If they catch me … A rusty fear strips my throat. Fuck, fuck, fuck. The front door is nailed shut and they've blocked the track to the beach. Where else can I go? I'll head back toward my bedroom. As I turn the corner, I'll roll off the balcony into the jungle. It's thick. It's tied in knots around the resort. There's no way they'll find me. I drop to a crouch and inch away from the edge, move low and quiet toward my room.

My legs are leaden – it's an effort to lift my feet.

And then I freeze.

There's the slap of rubber on wood. Coming from the direction of my bedroom. Coming toward me.

There's only one way left to go. The surf-check tower. I turn and launch up the rungs of the ladder two, three, four at a time, scramble across the platform into the darkest pool of shadow. And shake. Lace my hands together but still they shake. Fix my teeth together but still they make a porcelain chatter that the men will surely hear. It's over. They've seen me. They've heard me.

They're below me now, talking.

It doesn't sound like they've found Shane yet. I wonder if Shane is still at the front door. Or if he's hiding behind something, waiting to shoot. I wriggle to the edge of the platform on my belly and see four fishermen. None are looking up. The lights are on; the coiled bulbs gloss two of the men's hair. The other two wear skullcaps. There's the menace of murder taut in their spines, in the fingers that hold machetes. One circles the pool table, the rest are a little further back, closer to me.

Moments later I know why.

An explosion rocks the front of the resort.

I scream.

The four men have assembled in a line. Shane stumbles into view muttering incoherently. His hair is smeared across his face in wet, white-yellow streaks, except at his scalp line, where it's charred.

'Bajingan,' he jeers. 'You fucken Muslim bastards. Is that the worst you can do?' He cocks his gun.

The men look as if they're waiting for something, some kind of command. The two without skullcaps wear singlets. Their arms have the tight rubbery sinew of squid. The other two wear shirts. The backs of their shirts are starred with salty-shadows of sweat. It's four on one. Shane's hands wobble as he swings the gun from side to side. He knows if he shoots, the other three will be on to him.

There's a moment of waiting, when all is excruciatingly still, except for the low purr of a gecko preparing to sound. Ge-cko! Its voice pops. Ge-cko! And before its third call, two shadows move up behind Shane. The first holds a noosed fishing rope. The second holds a machete. With a swift measured throw, the first man looses the rope and it lands around Shane's neck. He gives the rope a jerk but Shane holds his ground. His monstrous arms fly out behind, in anger, in panic, in madness.

Ge-cko!

But Shane doesn't stand a chance. There's movement now, fast and wordless. These are men who know each other, who work together day in and day out on fishing boats, who no doubt face death in the black roll of the dry season swells. One of the men crushes his foot into Shane's balls. Another helps the man with the noose pull Shane to his back. A third leans down, certain and deadly, and lifts Shane's chin with the tip of his machete. He regards Shane dispassionately, as if he's about to fillet a fish.

I should stop watching. Should slide back from the edge of the platform. If Shane or any of the men look up, they'll see me. But I can't move. Not even a finger. It's like the dreams you have of being chased, and you can't run, the dreams of being buried, and you can't breathe. Fear has me locked to the wood, locked to the edge of the platform, locked to fate.

Shane looks up.

His face deforms with something malicious and coherent. His lips are starting to form words: he'll give me away to poach a few extra moments of life for himself.

As I recoil, he shouts hoarsely, 'Di atas! Ada perempuan di atas!'

Up there. There's a woman up there.

My heart thrashes. I slide to the furthest corner of the

platform, try to narrow myself into shadow, bite hard on the heel of my palm to stop from crying out, from crying. Maybe they won't believe Shane. Maybe no-one will come to check. There's nowhere for me to go. The ladder's the only way up and down. To my right, a palm tree curves its neck within leaping distance but if I miss it, I'll break my legs.

There's a wooden groan and the platform shifts ever so slightly. There's someone on the ladder. The rungs creak. One, two, three … Three heartbeats to a rung.

Suddenly, something small and furred cartwheels across the platform.

It's a monkey, wearing a red jacket.

A monkey, wearing the chilling half-moon mask of a doll's face.

Moments later, a young man's head appears. He has a set of those handsome cheekbones that distinguish the people here; those dark, stainless steel eyes. He must have been the one at the markets the other day, the one who followed me home after Dennis'. I wonder if he was also the one who saw me naked in the shower. I can't breathe. He's weighing me up. His eyes crawl from my sleep-tousled hair, to my breasts, to my pelvis, then back to my breasts. At last he meets my eyes. I plead with him through a look. Then whisper, 'Jangan.' Don't. He hesitates, undecided.

Below, the men are getting impatient, the fire is inching closer, they can feel it on their skin. It moves with languor, slowed by the moisture in the air, the sopping gutters, the vaporous palm fronds.

'Ada?' they call. 'Ada perempuan di sana? Ayo, cepat!'

He looks behind and below him.

For a moment the fire flashes against his cheekbone.

He looks back at me.

'Ada,' he says. There is. And he grabs my ankle.

I try to writhe away but he lifts his machete and nicks it against my leg. A quick bite of peroxide-white pain. A warning. I stop writhing. Scramble to my feet. Follow him down, not crying, not yet, but almost. The posters in the hallway are crimping and blackening. The men are arguing. Should they cut him up, cut off his balls, sever his head? Or should they leave him here, leave him to burn? The young man lets go of my wrist and steps forward to give Shane a passionate kick to the jaw.

'Cut off his head,' he says.

Blood appears at the corner of Shane's mouth.

The young man turns to me. 'Cut off both their heads.'

I start crying.

The young man slaps my face.

I barely feel it.

I'm thinking of Shane's head rolling yellow off the balcony; Shane's skin, spitting and bubbling like a white pig's.

Through my tears, I watch Shane, watch something snap – not Shane's sanity, that probably went years ago – but something else, perhaps the twin strangleholds of malaria and magic. For a big man on his back, he moves quick. He rams out his left leg and his foot connects with one of the men's shins. There's a sickening crunch and the fisherman falls backwards with a howl. Then Shane's on his feet, going hand over hand down the rope that's noosed his neck, hauling his captor toward him. His captor drops the rope and backs away, machete lifted uncertainly. Shane loosens the rope from his neck and starts swinging it, like a whip. It cracks across his captor's machete wrist; it cracks across his captor's crotch. The man nosedives, letting go of the machete and Shane pounces on it – burying the machete into the back of the man's thigh

242

with a sound like ruptured watermelon – and then jumps up again, grinning madly.

The other four have forgotten me and they're warily, hatefully, shifting their weight from foot to foot. Shane's facing them, legs apart and steady, a fishing rope in one hand, a machete in the other. Smoke turns through the air, gin and oranges, alternately clear and opaque. In minutes, it will be impossible to see anything. This is my chance. This might be my only chance. I squeeze my eyes shut for a split second. Then I spin and launch myself over the balcony rail.

65

Two of the bikes in the car park are in flames. My bike's okay – for the moment. I swing my leg over the hot vinyl and with a shaking hand force the key in the ignition.

It won't start.

'You motherfucker. Not now. Come on. Come on.'

The ignition switch isn't enough to get it going. The jungle around the side of the resort bends and breaks. They're coming. They're coming and I'm sitting here, bathed in the light of the fire. I kick the engine to life. It starts with a roar. I throw her into first, into second, into third; I'm out of there, racing into the tonic sting of night, no lights, no helmet, only fear.

The road is empty.

By the time I'm two thirds of the way to Ibu Ayu's, I still haven't passed a single truck, a single belching bus. I keep looking in my side mirror, expecting to see headlights behind me, but there's nothing. Perhaps they didn't follow me after all. Perhaps they went back to get Shane instead. I'll be at Ibu Ayu's in ten, in a car with a driver in fifteen, Bandar Lampung by late morning, Jakarta by evening. I'm gunna make it.

I swing a corner, almost skid out on a rash of loose gravel, steady the bike.

Now the last stretch of rice paddies before town. It's one of the worst parts of the road, with crater-like potholes that shift and slip every time it rains, making it impossible to memorise a clear track.

A single motorbike headlight appears in my side mirror. There's someone behind me. Maybe it's not them. Maybe it's someone out for a late-night drive.

The throttle won't twist any further. I can't seem to hold the bike steady, my hands are shaking too hard. I come unstuck on a pothole, feel myself vaulting over the handlebars, feel my lips and chin grazing rock and dried mud. Something kisses my hair. A fraction of a second later, two of the men from Shane's pass on a Honda Tiger. The young man with his monkey is holding a machete. He says something to his friend and the brake lights on the bike flash red. They're circling back for me.

I shut my eyes.

I have no more fight left.

Let it come down.

Nothing comes down. There's a truck rumbling toward me and the young men see it and flee. Back to Shane's. Back to finish him off. I touch my head.

My fingers lift a wet flap of scalp and hair.

66

At Ibu Ayu's I almost break down the wooden gate with my fists. It's locked.

'Bu! BU!'

There's a guard on the other side snoring warmly on his baton. I bang harder. 'PAK! PAK!'

'Apa?' a sleepy mumble.

My leg stings. My head stings. My heart tries to punch out my throat.

I have to get out of Batu Batur tonight. I have to get out of Batu Batur *right now*. They know where I am. They'll be back any minute for more.

'Come on, Pak!' I scream, throwing another closed fist at the gate.

'Ya, ya …'

He opens up. Did Ibu Ayu know something would happen tonight? Last time I came back late there was no guard, nor was the gate locked. She's walking toward me now, eyes full of sleep.

'Kok ribut sekali?' she complains. 'Ah, Penny! What is it?'

She's moving too slowly, everything is moving too slowly. I don't have time to explain. I point to my bleeding head. I point to my bleeding leg.

'Bu, I need to go. I need a driver. I need to leave Batu Batur right now. Sekarang, ya? Bandar Lampung, ya? Like, *right now!*'

67

On the road to Bandar Lampung I drift in and out of sleep. The pain in my head, despite popping four Panadol, still comes in surges. Outside the car, hypnotically beautiful strings of lights pool amber in the windowpanes of warungs and wartels. In every village, an immaculate white-tiled mosque resists the weary shadows of night and dust. I'm frightened by the flash of headlights against the back windscreen. I'm frightened they're following us. My stomach knots, my hands knot, my heart knots.

And we drive on.

Sometime near dawn we reach the outskirts of Bandar Lampung. And sometime near dawn I hear a small voice. I nearly jump off the back seat.

Behind me there's a headscarfed head.

'Penny?'

'Cahyati! What the – ?!'

'Maaf ya, Penny.' I'm sorry. 'But I thought I'd come with you to Lampung. I thought maybe you could buy me a ticket to Bali?'

She's so hopeful, so excited.

'Sure,' I manage to say at last. 'But I need to see a doctor first.'

My hair has glued to the cut and when I touch it, my fingers trace a damp lump.

Definitely a doctor first.

68

Six hasty stitches hold together the skin of my head after a trip to Bandar Lampung's biggest hospital. We catch the afternoon flight to Jakarta, and now I'm alone, in a bar on Jalan Jaksa. The temperature soars on dusk and stalls – everything is tensed to rain. I should be back in the room with Cahyati, trying to sleep, but despite the stitches and drugs, anxiety feels like it's about to rip open my chest. It's a crazy, desperate feeling, one I usually associate with betrayal, breakups or endings, though I know it's much bigger than Josh, or Matt, or even the last forty-eight hours; it's as if the whole month is about to burst from me and it either needs a target or to exhaust itself. The room Cahyati and I are sharing is no place to think of Shane on a darkly obsessive loop, it's no place to thrash, dry-throated with insomnia. Although it costs more than a night at Ibu Ayu's bungalows, it comes without towels, without sheets, without toilet paper, and toe prints crawl the walls. Cahyati was unfazed by the squalor and after our early dinner went straight back there to sleep, exhausted after a night bunched up in the back of the car.

The bar was a bad choice. It's filled with men who sit alone on stools. Their hands rest on the bar, starched with arthritis. I try to catch the eyes of the man closest but my loneliness, my desperation, is a repellent. He ignores me. A scrum of street kids trip past, with grasping fingers and too-big thongs. The coloured lights out the front dim and strain.

After a while, three young bules come in and sit up on stools at the table next to me. The guy is from Sweden, the girls are Australian. They've obviously just met because their conversation rings with the usual banal travel questions: how long have you been here? Where have you been? Where are you going? What do you do back home?

The Swedish bloke's on a six-month surfari, no doubt armed with a hair straightener and a formidable wardrobe. One of the girls is flying to Sulawesi on some youth development scholarship, and this is her first time out of the country. The other Aussie girl teaches Indonesian in Sydney. She's heading to Yogyakarta to kick off a ten-day refresher course at a language school. Although I'm bored with them already, I keep listening in, half-wishing they'll ask me to join them – just for the company. Anything would be better than the panic-reel in my head.

But they don't.

And really, what would I have in common with a pretty-boy Swede, an Indonesian teacher who's struggling to order her drink in the language she's supposed to teach, and a chick who looks just shy of thirty and has never left Australia? There's a terrible, yawning distance and the real trauma of last night (it was only last night!) churns somewhere beyond conscious thought, like there's judgement happening in a place within myself that's deep, mute, impossible to reach.

The sky opens, sending rain sluicing from the eaves.

I head back to the room, stumbling around puddles of oil, grease and Saturday night piss. I ease through the door quietly and peel off my wet clothes. Then I find a dry singlet and undies and lie on the skin-dusted mattress. There's a light on outside in the hall. It's bright enough to see fungi blooms on the ceiling and old spoors of kretek ash on the windowsill.

That's when I start to cry.

I wonder if they beheaded Shane, wonder what happened to the mean and hopelessly loyal Kristi, wonder what Matt will think when he finds out. I wonder if Franz and Adalie will unpack their boxes, whether the children will return to Dennis' class at school and what awaits Cahyati on the hard streets of Kuta. And I wonder again and again: what would've happened if I hadn't got away?

After a little while, a soft voice comes from across the room.

'Jangan sedih, Penny.' Don't be sad. And then in hesitant English, 'No worry, ya?'

That makes me cry even harder.

69

Cahyati spends the plane trip with her face pressed against the plexiglass, marvelling at the sprawl of Jakarta, at the volcanoes, the smoky drapes of Mount Bromo. Two friends meet her at the airport in Denpasar – they're girls from a village near Batu Batur. They'll probably whisk her off to a *kos* (a sort of shared house) where the three of them will stay in the one room, on the one mattress. I give her my number and promise to catch her through the week. I also slip her an extra hundred dollars and she looks dumbfounded.

As she glides off on the bike, sandwiched between the other girls, I find myself admiring her guts. It's a big deal for a young Sumatran girl. Does her mum know about it? And what will Ibu Ayu think when she finds out? The girls pass through the tollgate then turn left, down toward the tapering lanes of Tuban.

I pick a driver at the back of a pack of touts, the underdog, the one who hasn't raised his voice or seized my arm shouting, 'Yes, Miss! Yes, Miss! Kuta! Ubud! Lovina! Yes!' He takes my bags and we cut across the car park, climb into a white minivan. I'm starving. The taxi left Jalan Jaksa for the airport at four thirty this morning and we elbowed our way onto the six o'clock flight. The sweet, plastic-wrapped bun on the flight wasn't enough – I'm hungry for rice.

'Maaf ya, Pak. Boleh makan dulu?' I ask the driver.

'Where do you want to eat?'

'A good warung or rumah makan. Is there somewhere you'd recommend?'

The driver's eyelids droop for a moment then he nods.

We get talking, the usual questions. He's from Yogyakarta, which I'd guessed by his oval eyes and round face. He has a wife and four children here in Bali. His wife is Balinese but he moved here from Java as a twenty year old. After fifteen years of non-stop work he now almost owns outright the vehicle we're sitting in. He says the last few years have been hard though. Since the Bali bombing, Kuta's been too quiet, there aren't many tourists, it's nothing like it was before. People have lost their jobs, businesses have shut down, there are more children begging, there are people going hungry. Two of his friends died the night of the bombing. I murmur my sympathy.

Then he asks me where I'm from.

'Selandia Baru,' I lie, just to see how he'll respond.

'New Zealand, ya? That's good, I thought maybe you were Australian.'

'You don't like Australians?'

He gestures out the window. We're threading through one of Kuta's main arteries, under a riot of billboards advertising surf brands and fast food; we're passing windows full of tank-grown crustaceans, windows opening onto aquariums of Bintang bottles; we're passing hole-in-the-wall shops selling *Up the bum no babies* singlets.

'Australians own all of this,' he says. 'Australians think they own Bali!'

Ten minutes later, we're at a backstreet warung hovering over the best window spread of food I've seen in a month. It looks even better than the nasi campur at Pak Wu's. There're four types of fish, a lime green sambal, smoky chicken, chicken necks, a yellow chicken curry; there're beans and chilli, tempes and chilli, potatoes and chilli; there's diced eggplant and fried strings of water spinach.

'Please,' I gesture to the food. 'It's my shout.'

We sit together and eat with our fingers in silence.

When the driver finishes, he washes his hands and dries them carefully on a pink serviette. 'Did you know, Miss,' he says, 'in all the years I've been driving tourists around Bali, today was the first time a tourist asked me to sit down and share a meal.'

70

A week later, on Boxing Day, the warungs of Kuta are filled with hysterical buzz. Televisions are switched to news. A tsunami has swallowed Banda Aceh. Thousands are dead. The only things left standing, in stark exclamation, are the coconut trees and mosques. Some of the tourists head straight up the Bukit Peninsula, the hill closest to Kuta with its natural barrier of cliffs. Others jump on bikes and rip up to Ubud, the tourist town tucked among rice paddies and jungle where the Frenchman went to do yoga. I stay glued to the television with the staff at the losmen.

71

The days fall into a pattern. I sleep late. Drink coffee. And after 2pm, I wander the noodle-narrow lanes through Legian until I find a bar I like. For the last few afternoons and evenings I've been drinking and smoking kreteks at a place that's quiet and advertises cheap arak. The staff leave me alone to watch the Indonesian news on TV and it doesn't fill up with bules until later at night. I haven't got in touch with any of my old school friends or started looking for another job. My head's healing and my frayed nerves are under control; at least enough for me not to jump.

I've been drifting, drinking, breaking.

I half expect to run into Josh and Jessica. Knowing Josh, they probably stayed in one of those flash resorts down at Nusa Dua. Or maybe they are back in Perth by now, finding a rhythm with each other: taking long runs together on the weekends, downing post-coital piccolo lattes. I keep thinking I should be relieved. After that night with Matt I decided it was off. Decided my heart had cooled. But I don't feel relieved, just betrayed. Not so much by Josh, but by his perception of me: no plans, never fully present, a drifter. Maybe he's right, but still, I can't help but feel like there must be another way to live, a way where those paradoxical moments of profound sadness and rapture hit you daily. There's something intoxicating about living in extreme places, among extreme people. You never, for a moment, forget that you are alive.

72

Cahyati texts to say she's landed a job at a bar in Legian and asks me to drop in. I've passed the bar a hundred times in the last week but never stepped inside. The pool tables, dance floor and the listless Javanese beauties at the bar suggest the place is a pick-up joint, not somewhere a single white Aussie girl would be particularly welcome.

From the moment I walk in, the girls ignore me and the owner eyeballs me.

I almost don't recognise Cahyati. She's abandoned the headscarf and crafted her hair into a perfect black afro. Her skin is glossy with coconut oil and she sways a little uncertainly in indigo heels. Compared to the other girls here, with their tattoos and cigarettes, all suspiring the smoky smell of sex, Cahyati has a complete, naïve grace, a complete lack of pretension or cunning.

I feel like throwing up. Does she have any idea of what's *really* expected of her here? This is my fault. I bought her a ticket to Bali. Of course this would happen.

'So what do you have to do?' I ask.

'Talk to bule, get them drinks. It's pretty easy really! So much better than everyday cooking, everyday laundry, everyday yelled at by Ibu Ayu. Sometimes they touch me, here, here, but the girls say it's all part of the job. It doesn't mean anything.'

I almost choke. 'Well, make sure you send me a text if I can help at all. A place to stay, money for food, a ticket home in case you don't like it ...'

She waves away my offers. 'I like it,' she says. 'So Penny, how long you stay in Bali?'

'I dunno.' When I shift the darkness in my head. When my money runs out. When I get a better offer.

We exchange a few more awkward words until the Australian owner, hairy hands flat on the bar, glares me out.

73

Emile emails. The Frenchman. He tells me he's in Banda Aceh shooting the aftermath of the tsunami. Staying at the Sultan. He tells me they need translators, like, *right now*, that I should stop drinking gin and tonics at Shane's and come and do some real work. I haven't heard from Emile since Ibu Ayu's, and given the chaos and conditions in Banda Aceh I'm amazed he even managed to get an email off to me, more amazed that he *chose* to get in touch.

My first thought is no way. Working in post war zones, post natural disaster zones, leads to madness, sadness, suicide. I haven't forgotten the Frenchman's anguished eyes. He knew as well as I that a two-week yoga course in Ubud wouldn't assuage his grief, wouldn't wipe the memories. Not so soon, anyway.

Aceh is all everyone's been talking about.

They're saying a peace agreement will be reached between the government and GAM. They're saying the tsunami has been a blessing, because it's meant the end of the war. Side by side, soldiers and GAM guerrilla fighters dig graves. Most of the dead are women. Is this what it takes, to soften indoctrination in the hearts of radicals, to remember our shared humanity? Should a tsunami hit Batu Batur, would Shane be out there with his neighbours, clearing the debris, lifting bodies out of the mud?

I think of Shane's tattoo, a throwback to the early independence slogans lobbed at the Dutch and strangely prophetic.

Merdeka atau Mati. Freedom or Death. I think about my options.

Remember I'm living, by choice, on a faultline.

Realise for these people, for so many people, there is no choice.

I write to Emile and tell him I'm on my way.

74

It's my last night in Kuta. Cahyati's offered to give me a lift to the airport in the morning. I'm working my way steadily through a jug of arak laced with honey and lime. A television screen reels a mute, anxious blue. The boys sitting across the road selling sunglasses yell, 'Transport!' every time a hot Scandinavian chick in tiny shorts walks past. European expatriates, their faces tanned tense, look put out by having to come this far south of Seminyak. Australian girls with braids and Bintang singlets shuffle slow sunburnt legs. There's the constant buzz of motorbikes and the bright patter of business.

I swirl the arak around my mouth.

Dusk slowly disinfects the sun's bite. Everyone will be on the beach for sunset and they'll get a cracker – it rained all morning and now has cleared to a breezy blue.

As darkness falls, the bar fills with Aussies. I've lost a sense of time, have brushed off a couple of long-toothed Pommies hunting for a root and am deep in thought about Batu Batur. Suddenly, through the white noise of drunk Aussies, I hear the word 'Shane'. At first I think I've imagined it, think the sound has manifested itself from the dreamy depths of my thought. Then I hear his name again, cutting hard through the glassy distance of arak, and it takes a few moments to switch in, a few more moments to realise the guy isn't talking about one of his mates. A bloke behind me is talking about Sumatran Shane. *Shane* Shane. I twist around.

At first I think it's the same group of guys who were at the resort. Then I look closer and realise it isn't Johnno, Andy and Rob. Different faces, same Australian surf froth. One of the guys says he heard something about a fire. Something about Shane being taken to hospital by his housekeeper for severe burns. He says that when they got him there, after treating him for the burns, the doctors found something really unusual. Only one of the doctors had ever seen a case like it and that had been fifty years ago, when he was first training.

He'd never seen anything like it since.

'Well for fuck's sake Scotty, don't keep us hanging.'

'You're not gunna believe this, but they found all this shit in his gut. Bits of hair and mirror and broken glass. They've pumped it out, they say he'll live, but ...'

I swivel back to face the street. It's started to drizzle. Had it worked, the spell? Or was it just another bit of Indo rumour?

I put my glass down. I don't know if I'm glad Shane's alive. Don't know if he deserves to have survived. Do know there's a measure of relief creeping into my heart. If Shane is alive then his attackers are either dead or waiting for him. If *he's* alive then they are not coming for me.

It must be after midnight, because here's the dog man, limping down the lane. He has a bamboo pole over his shoulders, a steel food pot of curried dog on either side. He taps a spoon against a bowl and cries, 'Anjing, anjing, anjing.'

I slip out of my seat and follow him.

Acknowledgements

I've punished hundreds of people over the past eight years on various aspects of *Troppo*. A special thank you to Tom, who has shared every disappointment and delight on this long journey. Thank you to Bruce McDowall, for Dovlatov, Bukowski, *Blood Meridian* and Beckett, and for his reassurance that at twenty-nine, while I won't become 'Miss Cable Beach', I am 'holding the line'. Thank you to Alan Wearne, for introducing me to the gorgeous prose of Antonio Lobo Antunes and for sending crazily eclectic reading lists every few months. Alan also put me in touch with the esteemed poet Geoffrey Lehmann, who kindly allowed me to quote sections of an early version of his wonderful, powerful poem 'New Guinea Episode'. I am lucky also to have a bunch of brutal critics, starting with Felix Prael. Many years ago, Felix patiently read and edited dozens of my short stories and poems and always gave unflinching criticism. More recently, thank you to my mum, dad, my sister Charlotte, Josh, Elisa, Gilly, Tilly, Luke, Marco, Anna, Jess, Jemma, Shady, Jacqueline, Ibu Santi, Pak Waway, Pak Nana, Marie and Bill for their input on early drafts of *Troppo*. Georgia Richter from Fremantle Press has been a pleasure to work with on the final drafts, and has helped transform this rough gem of a manuscript into a proper novel. Finally, I would like to thank Ibu Yeti and Pak Omay, for allowing Tom and me to rent their beautiful home in Batu Karas, a small fishing village in West Java. They welcomed us wholeheartedly into their community during the drafting of *Troppo*.

A note on language usage in this novel: in Bahasa Indonesia, words do not take an 's' to form a plural. Westerners (bule) do not always adhere to this practice. A glossary of Indonesian words and phrases used in *Troppo* accompanies the teaching and book club notes for this book, and can be downloaded from fremantlepress.com.au.

Madelaine Dickie

Madelaine Dickie has worked as a rollerblading and skate-boarding instructor, a radio producer and a disability-support officer. Most recently, she's managed the media and communications for an Aboriginal organisation in the Kimberley, Western Australia. Work means travel – travel means surfing! Madelaine's scored empty point breaks in Mozambique, got crook with malaria in Indonesia, crashed a rental car racing to the surf in Spain, and has been bewitched by welwitschia in Namibia. It's always easier to write when you're on the road. In 2011, Madelaine received a Prime Minister's Australia Asia Endeavour Award to move to West Java, Indonesia, and complete her first novel, *Troppo*. In 2014, *Troppo* won the City of Fremantle T.A.G. Hungerford Award.